WAR AT THE SNOW WHITE MOTEL

and OTHER STORIES

WAR
AT THE
SNOW WHITE
MOTEL

and OTHER STORIES

TIM WYNNE-JONES

Groundwood Books
House of Anansi Press
Toronto Berkeley

Copyright © 2020 by Tim Wynne-Jones
Published in Canada and the USA in 2020 by Groundwood Books

"The Journey to Ompah" was originally published in *Like Father, Like Son?*,
edited by Tony Bradman (Kingfisher Books, 2006). "In a House Built Out of
Dragonfly Wings" was originally published in *Beyond the Rainbow Warrior*,
edited by Michael Morpurgo (Greenpeace & Pavilion Books, 1996). "Christmas with Auntie Annie Ping-Pong" was originally published in *All in the
Family: Stories that Hit Home*, edited by Tony Bradman (A & C Black, 2008).

Groundwood Books / House of Anansi Press
groundwoodbooks.com

We gratefully acknowledge for their financial support of our publishing
program the Canada Council for the Arts, the Ontario Arts Council and the
Government of Canada.

 Canada Council Conseil des Arts
for the Arts du Canada

 ONTARIO ARTS COUNCIL
CONSEIL DES ARTS DE L'ONTARIO
an Ontario government agency
un organisme du gouvernement de l'Ontario

With the participation of the Government of Canada
Avec la participation du gouvernement du Canada | Canada

Library and Archives Canada Cataloguing in Publication
Title: War at the Snow White Motel and other stories / Tim Wynne-Jones
Other titles: Short stories. Selections
Names: Wynne-Jones, Tim, author.
Description: Includes 6 new and 3 previously published stories.
Identifiers: Canadiana (print) 20190155353 |
Canadiana (ebook) 20190155361 | ISBN 9781773060477 (hardcover) |
  ISBN 9781773060484 (EPUB) | ISBN 9781773060491 (Kindle)
Classification: LCC PS8595.Y59 A6 2020 | DDC jC813/.54—dc23

Jacket and interior design by Michael Solomon
Jacket art by Byron Eggenschwiler

Groundwood Books is committed to protecting our natural environment.
This book is made of material from well-managed FSC®-certified forests,
recycled materials, and other controlled sources.

Printed and bound in Canada

MIX
Paper from
responsible sources
FSC
www.fsc.org
FSC® C016245

This book is for my writing amigos: Ken Oppel, Richard Scrimger and Arthur Slade. The next round's on me, guys.

CONTENTS

"When you get to the top of the mountain,
keep climbing."
— Zen saying

WAR AT
THE SNOW WHITE MOTEL

IT'S AUGUST the fourth, 1964, and we're spending the night at the Snow White Motel in Vermont. We're on our way from Ottawa to Maine for a vacation. Dad's gone into the office, which is through a bright red door in Snow White's yellowy-gold dress. The top part of Snow White towers above the office. She's wearing her black vest and puffy blue sleeves and that high white collar just like in the Disney movie, and she has her hands up to either side of her head in surprise, which is easy to understand. It would be pretty surprising having people coming in and out of your dress all day long.

Dad's taking a long time. I stare at the vacancy sign on the lawn. It's Doc the Dwarf holding a wooden plaque, but there's a little flap before the word "Vacancy." I guess that behind that flap is the word "No." So why is Dad taking so long? Maybe there's a skill-testing question? You can't stay at the motel unless you can name all the dwarfs. Maybe he needs my help?

"Do you think Dad needs my help?" I ask Mum.

"No, Rex, you just stay put," she says.

"I don't know why Dad won't let us get out," says Annie Oakley. She's drooping beside me and just as sweaty as I am.

"It's because of the highway," says Mum.

"It's a pretty poky highway," says Annie. "What does he think I'm going to do, run out in the middle of it?"

"Yes, probably," says Mum.

"Which would make more room back here," I say and get a pointy elbow right in the ribs.

"Oww!"

"I hope we get to stay in the Sleepy cabin," says Flora Bella, yawning.

"Will Snow White come and kiss us good night?" asks Rupert. He sounds a little scared.

He's kneeling on the front seat looking up at Snow White, who is smiling down on the parking lot. One of her fingers is missing at the first knuckle. There's bird poop on her shoulder and the paint is peeling on her right cheek, which makes it look as if she's got acne.

Mum hugs Rupert. "I'm not sure," she says. "But I certainly will." Then she gives him a good tickle. She is so happy to be on holiday. I am, too, but I'm sure tired of being in this car on a hot August afternoon. We've been on the road since before it got light.

There's only the four of us kids, this time. My two older sisters stayed home because they have summer jobs. It's sort of too bad, because Letitia would have loved this place. She kind of lives in a fairy tale, even though she's sixteen. Always dreaming that someday her prince will come.

"Is the prince in Snow White Charming or is that Cinderella's guy?" I ask.

"I think so," says Mum.

"Barf," says Annie Oakley. She hates fairy tales and princesses and princes and ... well, pretty well everything. Especially me.

Finally, Dad comes out of the office holding up two keys attached to wooden dwarfs. Hooray!

We tumble out of the car and Dad hands Annie a key. It's Grumpy. Perfect.

"You two will have to share a cabin," he says to me and Annie. Not perfect.

"What?" says Annie. She makes it sound like he just told us the cabin was a snake pit.

"I don't think that's a good idea," I say.

"You can say that again," says Annie. "But don't!" She makes a fist at me.

"Now, now, you two," says Mum. "It's just for one night."

My last night on Earth, I find myself thinking.

I SNEEZE as soon as I step through the doorway.

"It's not Sneezy," says Annie Oakley. "You're so stupid."

"Sorry," I say.

"Not as sorry as you're going to be if you step across this line," says Annie. She's plucked a bunch of fake flowers from a vase on the windowsill and is placing them in a line splitting the room in half, with one twin bed on one side and one twin bed on the other. There aren't many flowers. It's not much of a wall. But when she finishes, she turns and glares at me.

"What about the bathroom?" I ask.

The door is right in the middle.

"Good idea," she says. "You can sleep in there!"

"I just meant —"

"I know what you meant," she says and marches along the line of flowers, growling like a tiger in a cage who'd give anything to get out and eat me.

I shake my head wearily and go sit on my bed. It's got a Grumpy comforter on it. Meanwhile, Annie has grabbed her bathing suit from her suitcase and gone into the bathroom to change. She slams the door. There's a little desk on my side of the room with a wooden chair. For just a moment I think of sticking the back of that chair under the bathroom doorknob, like they do in movies so that the person in the other room can't get out. But Annie would get out, even if she had to knock the whole door down. And then it really would be my last night on Earth.

THE SWIMMING pool is shaped like a heart. No, wait — it's an apple. Of course! The poisonous apple Snow took a bite of that sent her into a coma. Sort of weird, really, when you think about it. Who'd want to swim in a poisonous pool? No one by the look of it. The pool is empty. All that

17

delicious coolness just lying there, sparkling in the late afternoon sun.

There's music coming from somewhere, Top 40 radio. Right now it's "The Shoop Shoop Song." There are a few people tanning on their towels or sitting in deck chairs, soaking up the sun. No one from my family other than Annie. She's walking around the pool with her arms tight across her chest, glaring at the water as if it's filled with alligators and she's trying to decide which one she's going to wrestle first.

Poison or not, alligators or not, I'm hot and I want into that pool. I head straight for the diving board, take as big a bounce as I can off the end and cannonball into the water.

Splash!

I drift down into the blue coolness, my eyes wide open. *Glug, glug, glug.* There is only watery sunlight down here, as if the sun was a big yellow china ball that someone smashed into little shards and sprinkled on the blue tile floor. My goggles aren't on tight enough and water seeps inside, so with a little kick off the bottom I drift to the surface.

"Hey, you!"

A voice booms above me. I grab the lip of the pool. I also grab a mouthful of water, which makes me cough and cough. There is a large pair of hairy feet planted right beside my hand. My vision is all swimmy as I look up through goggles full of water — way up, past a pair of Superman legs, a pair of yellow bathing trunks with palm trees on them, a chest big enough to pitch a tent on — to a face glaring down at me as if I am a toad and the only thing stopping him from squashing me is that he doesn't have his toad-squashing boots on. Then I see the comic book in his hand. It's sopping wet.

"What do you think you're doing?" he shouts.

I'm coughing up a lung. That's what I'm doing! If I were smart, I'd let go of my hold, sink into the deep end and drown.

Now another guy joins the first. They're both teenagers, the first with a blond buzz cut and the other with squirrely black hair. They're wearing shades and glaring at me. "The Shoop Shoop Song" has finished. In the background, Ray Orbison is singing "It's Over."

"I asked you a question," says Buzzcut.

"You got a brain in your head?" says Squirrel.

I cough up some more of the pool and Squirrel steps back as if I'm going to throw up on his feet. Meanwhile, Buzzcut squats down so he's as near to me as he can get. He's poised like he's a catcher and my head is a fastball he's going to whip to second base as soon as he gets his hands on it.

"See this?" he says. He holds up the soaking comic book. It's *Strange Tales*.

Squirrel squats beside him. "He asked you if you saw what you did, brat."

I nod and gulp and Buzzcut swats me over the head with the soaking comic book. Once, twice, three times.

"Did you stop to look what you was doing?" shouts Buzzcut. "You ever think about anyone but yourself? What are you, some kinda … some kinda depth charge?"

It's a lot of questions and he hasn't stopped hitting me with the soggy comic. All I can do is avert my eyes and hunch my shoulders and take it, while little wet ragged bits of Captain America fall all around me.

Slap, slap, slap!

"Yeah," says Squirrel, when Buzzcut finally stops to take a breath. "You got any idea what's going on here?"

No, I think. No idea at all. And that's when I see what they can't see: Annie Oakley sneaking up behind them. She glares at me not to look at her and so I look at Buzzcut and blurt out, "I'm sorry."

"As if my life ain't bad enough," says Buzzcut. "Jeez, Louise!"

Meanwhile, Annie has slipped out of her yellow flip-flops and she's raising her right foot. *No*, I want to shout but —

Wham!

I duck just in time, as Buzzcut goes barreling over my head into the pool.

"What the —"

And —

Bam!

Squirrel's next.

I don't wait around to see what happens. I clamber out of the pool and take off toward the cabin named Grumpy. Then I stop and turn around.

The guys are shouting, "No, no! Don't! Don't!"

Annie's standing right on the edge of the pool with their transistor radio in her hands, holding it high above the water. I'm fifty yards away but I swear I can see the evil gleam in her eyes. I turn and beat it back to the cabin while the Beatles sing "A Hard Day's Night."

"They're going to kill you, you know."

I'm sitting on my bed, staring across the borderline of plastic flowers at my fourteen-year-old sister, who's sitting on her bed scowling back at me.

"Not if they know what's good for them," she says.

"I don't think they do," I say.

"That's their problem," she says.

"That's just it. Now it's our problem, too."

She shrugs.

"Are you really not one bit frightened?"

She squinches up her face and it's a bit of a give-away. She is. But she's not going to show it, let alone say it. I sigh and shake my head. This could end up being a really hard day's night. "I sure hope they didn't see which cabin we're in."

She shrugs. "They try anything, they'll wish they didn't," she says. But then she gets up and walks to the window over the desk and pokes open the curtain. She's nervously clenching and unclenching the fist of her free hand. I don't bother telling her she crossed into my half of the room.

THE FAMILY heads out to a diner across the highway from Snow White. The diner is called Hansel and Gretel's. We just follow the bread crumbs across the road.

"Maybe there will be fattened-up little children

to eat for dinner," I say to baby Rupert.

"I hope not," he says.

"Stop that, Rex," says Mom. "What's gotten into you?"

I glance at Annie Oakley, who glares back at me.

We don't ever eat out except on holidays and I can have anything I want, so I order a cheeseburger, onion rings, fries and a large root beer. I can't wait. I can already tell from the aroma of fat in Hansel and Gretel's that it's going to be a great dinner.

And then suddenly it's not.

Out the window I see Buzzcut and Squirrel heading over from Snow White right toward the diner. Buzzcut's got his hands deep in the pockets of his Bermudas and Squirrel's talking to him, like he's trying to cheer him up. Buzzcut sure looks like he needs cheering up.

"Did you see —"

But Annie pokes me in the ribs with her pointy elbow. I swallow my "Ow!" and glance her way. She saw them, all right.

"They'll have to climb over you to get at me," she whispers, hot in my ear.

"That's what I was afraid of," I say.

The pretty blonde waitress who took our orders greets Buzzcut and Squirrel at the door. "Hi,

Skip," she says. "Hi, Baxter." Her name, Penny, is embroidered onto a badge on her chest. Her hair is in a ponytail and her eyes are blue and she gives Skip a peck on the cheek. And as pretty as she is, even that doesn't lighten his mood.

I grab a menu and hide behind it as Penny leads them right past our table. Luckily, the menu is really big. Unluckily, it's not big enough. Baxter steps on my foot as they pass.

"Oh, sorry," he says.

I swallow my "Ow!" again. Maybe "Ow!" is all I'm going to get to eat tonight. When they've passed, I turn around in time to see Skip turn and scowl at Annie.

"Don't ogle, Rex," says Mum.

I turn back. Dad's disappeared. His head, anyway. It's behind the newspaper. Mum's busy with the baby, Flora Bella is coloring the menu with crayon flowers and I don't want to even look at Annie. So I end up reading the front page of the newspaper Dad's hiding behind. I don't read newspapers much, but the headlines grab my eye and before I know it, I'm reading everything.

Then dinner comes and by now I'm kind of full. Full of worries about Skip and Baxter. Full of worries about the world.

"What's wrong with you, Soldier?" says Dad, spying my untouched plate.

"Nothing," I say and start eating just so he doesn't ask any more questions. But my head is spinning over what I read. I turn around and Penny is sitting next to Skip in his booth, her hand resting tenderly on his arm. He looks sad and angry.

Mum and Dad talk quietly between themselves. Well, Dad talks and Mum says, "Really?" And, "Oh, that must be terrible." And, "I couldn't bear that. Poor woman." I don't get much of what Dad says, because he's mumbling from behind his paper, but I know what I'm going to do when we get back to Grumpy.

Skip ends up leaving alone before his order even arrives, both hands shoved in his shorts as if there's something important in there he doesn't want to lose. I watch him cross the parking lot, then stop and glance back. Annie Oakley's watching his every move. He shakes his head at her and points two fingers at his eyes and then at her. Not a good sign. Annie mumbles something threatening and returns to her dinner, slicing up her food as though it's the enemy. I watch Skip head toward Snow White, open the red door and head into the office. Snow White throws up her arms in surprise. "Oh, my!" she seems to be saying.

Baxter stays and ends up with two dinners. Every now and then, he looks up from his food and sneers at us. One time he slices his hand across his neck.

"Uh-oh," I mumble.

Penny has to work, but she looks like she caught whatever it is that's eating Skip. At one point I notice her leaning on another waitress's shoulder, crying. Maybe she and Skip broke up. I hate to see her sad, but in one way that would be great. I could stay behind when my parents left tomorrow morning, and when I was eighteen, I could ask Penny out on a date. It'd be a long wait, but I'm a pretty patient person.

WE'RE GOING to get an early start and be in Ocean Park by daybreak. Assuming we make it through the night.

I ask Mum and Dad if I can sleep on the floor in their cabin. They got Happy. There he is, on a painted board above their doorway. With his roly-poly belly and his roly-poly cheeks and that big cheery grin.

"Please, Mum. It's important."

"Talk to him," says Mum to Dad.

"Soldier," says Dad, with his hand on my shoulder. "There are a lot worse things than an older sister, let me tell you."

"Annie Oakley isn't really my sister. I think you stole her from the zoo."

"We didn't steal her from anywhere and I'm afraid she is."

"Yeah, well that makes two of us."

Dad sighs. "I'm not even going to ask what she did now," he says. "But I'll admit she doesn't always think of the consequences of her actions."

"Like getting us killed," I say. I start to walk away up the hill toward Grumpy. "Have a great time in Ocean Park," I call back to Mom and Dad. "I'll be thinking of you from my grave."

"Rex." I don't stop. "Rex!" says Dad more sharply. And so I head back down to him, my chin on my chest.

"What's going on, Soldier?" he says.

So I tell him everything.

BACK IN Grumpy, I turn on the TV. They get more channels than we do back in Canada, but wherever I look it's the news, and I sit and watch. Luckily, Annie's not there. Maybe she's smartened

27

up and gone home. It'd be a long walk but not as long as being dead. I turn off the television. By the time the image disappears to nothing, I've made a big decision.

He's going to get us. Skip. The only way is to strike first. Catch him off guard.

I walk over to my little suitcase. There's nothing much in it but shorts and underwear and bathing suits and T-shirts and more shorts. But there are a couple of valuable things. I open the case, take a deep breath. They're the only weapons I've got. I'm just not sure I'm brave enough to use them.

I walk down the hill toward Snow White. From the back she looks eerie in the fading light. The spotlights have come on out front and from my point of view she's just a huge silhouette with her arms flung upward in shock. From here, she could be a witch.

As I crunch across the gravel of the parking lot, I notice they've uncovered the "No" sign. That means there are no vacancies at the Snow White Motel. But they may have acted too soon. If what I have planned doesn't work out, Grumpy may be available, once they clean up all the gore and mess from our dead bodies. I stop at the red door and consider going back. Or better still, knocking on the Happy cabin and demanding that my parents take me in. They have to do that when your life's in danger.

But no. I have to do this.

I hope he's still here. Skip. He's the owner's son. That's what Dad told me. I take a deep breath and open the door and he's there, all right. He's sitting at a desk behind the counter. He looks up with a smile.

"I'm sorry, there are no …" he says before he recognizes me, then the smile disappears. "What do you want?" he says. I just stand there on the threshold. He can't beat me to death here, can he? It wouldn't be very good for business to have blood splattered all over the place. "Well?" he says.

I get my feet to move and I walk up to the counter. "Here," I say and try to hand him my almost brand-new Panasonic transistor radio in its leather carrying case.

"What is this?"

"It's to replace the one my sister threw in the pool." He looks at it, doesn't touch it. "Take it," I say. He frowns at me. "It's not booby-trapped."

He reaches out and picks it up by the strap and swings it around to look at it.

"It's an RF-811," I say.

29

He nods. Then looks hard at me. "Is it hers?"

I shake my head. "No, it's mine."

He nods, looks the radio over one more time and then puts it back on the counter. "She never threw it in," he says.

What? How did I miss that?

"If it were hers, I'd-a kept it, anyway," says Skip. "But you didn't do anything."

"She was just defending me. She doesn't always think before she acts."

"Yeah, well, she wouldn't be the only one," he says. "Now beat it."

Beating it is a really good idea. Except I can't move. "I did do something," I say. "I gave your comic a soaker. That was a really good issue. 'The Thing is here!'" I say, putting on my best Boris Karloff voice. "'The Thing has us trapped! There's no place to run!'"

He screws up his face. "You're weird, little man," he says. "Now get out of here." He looks down at the motel registry book open in front of him. "You're in Grumpy, right?" He looks up. I nod. "Have a good night, Rex," he says. His voice is tired, not really angry. Just kind of drained, worn out.

Still I don't move. Can't. I take back the transistor and put the strap over my shoulder. But I've got something else, something I've been keeping hidden from him behind the counter. My only other weapon. Now I lift it up. "I owe you this," I say and reluctantly shove a rolled-up comic his way.

He takes it and unscrolls it to look at the cover. His eyes grow wide. "It's the new *Strange Tales*," he says. "This only just came out.

"Whoa!" he says, flipping through the pages.

"It's got the Human Torch, Doctor Strange and Thor in it," I say.

"And Thing," he adds.

"Yeah, and Thing. It's … it's yours," I say.

He frowns at me, bobs his head up and down, and purses his lips as if he's coming to a big decision. Then he smiles. Phew! I want to ask him if that means we're square now, and he won't come and kill us in our sleep. Then again, I don't want to give him any ideas.

"Thanks, kid. I'm going to take you up on this."

"Okay," I say. Now I should definitely turn around and go but I can't. I'm still not finished.

"I'm really sorry," I say.

"Yeah, well … I'm sorry, too. I kinda lost it up there."

"No, I mean about, you know, the war." Now the sadness seeps back into his eyes and his expression grows hard again. Uh-oh. "I didn't know they just declared war," I say. "Today."

He leans on the desk behind the counter and looks away. His face is bitter. "They didn't 'declare' war," he says. "They just started a war with no declaration or nothing."

I don't say anything. All I know from Dad is that Skip just registered with Selective Services a few days back. That's what Dad told me. He got talking with Skip's dad when he was checking in. That's what took so long.

A boy has to register within thirty days of his eighteenth birthday and Skip had done it right away, like a good citizen. He didn't know then that they'd go right out and start a war, as if they'd just been waiting for him. Which means he might have to go over there, wherever it is. I'm not sure. I saw a map of Vietnam on the news. It looked like a long snaky "S" with a beehive hairdo.

"You'd better get to bed, Rex. You're leaving real early, from what I hear."

"Okay." Finally, my feet unlock and I turn to go. I'm relieved, I guess, but not happy.

"Hey, Rex," Skip says. I turn around at the door. "I might not get drafted," he says. I nod. "It could all be over real soon."

"I hope so," I say.

I walk up the hill, feeling a little bit better, even though I'd had to give up a brand-new comic I'd been saving until we got to the cottage. I look over toward Happy. Dad's standing outside under the porch light smoking his pipe.

I head up toward him.

"How goes the war, Soldier?" he says.

ANT AND
THE PRAYING MANTIS

PRETTY WELL everybody has some kind of creature in their name. There are eight people in my class with ants in their name and four people with bees. There's also Marybeth Stone who has both an ant and a bee in her name, which maybe accounts for how twitchy she is. There's also a cow, an eel, a flea and a rat in our class. I'm not saying everybody lives up to their creature name, but some do. Take Dierdre Prosser, for instance. She has a spider in her name and she is most definitely spidery: a gossip girl always weaving webs.

My name is Ant. Well, Anthony Lawson, but my creature name is Ant and I'm fine with that. Ants are industrious. Stubborn. They can lift a hundred times their weight, right up over their heads. They are superheroes. I made a T-shirt in summer camp with a line of ants that look as if they're coming out of my left pant pocket, meandering across my torso, over my shoulder and marching all the way down to my right back pocket. Ants with a goal.

Sometimes your creature name is just sitting right there, like mine is. Sometimes it's hidden and you have to move letters around to find it. So if your name is, say, Vera Best, you could go a long, long time never even realizing you had a beaver hiding secretly in your name. I thought she'd be excited to know about it. I was wrong.

"Hey, you," says the new girl. "Do you have any idea how creepy this is?"

"What?"

"Calling people names."

New Girl looms over me like a tree in winter, all shivering limbs.

"I didn't call anybody a name."

"Yes, you did," says New Girl. Behind her, a few paces off, there's a gaggle of girls and one of them is crying. Vera Best.

"Oh," I say, confused. "I didn't call her anything."

"You did so!" shouts Vera.

"No, I didn't, honest." I look past New Girl at Vera. "All I did was tell you what I'd found in your name."

"In front of a bunch of people," says Vera.

"And now everyone is calling her … calling her that," says New Girl, stepping in front of me to protect Vera from having to so much as see me.

"Everyone?" It's the first I've heard of it.

"Some people," says New Girl, glaring down at me.

"Is that my fault?" I ask. And it really is a question.

"What do you think?" says New Girl.

I'm not sure what I think. I'm not very fast on my feet. Ants just aren't. "I didn't mean to hurt her feelings."

"She's not some animal," says New Girl. "So just stop it, okay?"

New Girl doesn't wait for my answer. She turns and joins the gaggle of girls and they scuttle away, with their arms around Vera, throwing angry glances back my way.

I thought Vera would be excited to have a creature name. Meryl Squires loved it when I told her she had a squirrel in her name. And Rose Campione told me she was going to get a tattoo of a scorpion when she was old enough. I think it's magic how words are full of other words. I stand there feeling angry. Well, angry and sorry and really stupid.

SAMANTHA GRIMSBY-PAINE. That's the new girl's name. It's kind of an amazing name and she is kind of amazing. So tall and willowy.

"*Qué es* 'willowy'?" says Moth.

So I try to explain to him that Samantha is tall, but she moves kind of gracefully and her long crinkly hair is like the fronds of a willow tree. Except not green.

Moth frowns. "She just looks *desgarbada* to me," he says. Then he finds the English word. "Gawky."

He's right, I guess; she is kind of gawky. But apart from her biting my head off like that for something I didn't mean to do, she's kind of cool … well, in a slightly frightening way. I don't say that to Moth.

Moth's real name is Timoteo Hiraldo, which is about as good a name as you could ever want. Except he doesn't like it. Why? Because people at our school call him Timmy.

"Timmy," he said, when we first were getting to know each other. Then he gagged.

"So, how about 'Moth'?" I said.

"Qué es 'moth'*?"* So I told him. "Ah," he said, smiling. *"Una polilla."* He seemed okay about having a moth in his name. *"Una mariposa nocturna,"* he said.

Even I could translate that: a butterfly of the night. His eyes glowed as if he was picturing a superhero with colorful wings instead of a cape. And so we became Ant and Moth. Just a couple of little insects trying to get through middle school without being stepped on or swatted.

SAMANTHA GRIMSBY-PAINE: she's got an ant in her name, just like me, and a manta ray, which is ultracool. Talk about graceful. I see those two creatures right off. But it's only when I get home from school that day and I'm doodling with all the possibilities of all those letters that I figure out just how amazing her name is.

"DON'T YOU ever learn!?" says Samantha Grimsby-Paine at lunch the very next day. She plants a Post-it Note on my chest so hard she almost knocks me over. "This was sticking on my locker. Half the school saw it before I did!"

I look down at the note. I can't see what it says upside down, but it isn't my writing. I peel it off and read it.

Beware the Preying Mantis!!!

"I didn't do this," I say.

"Really?"

"I told you about it this morning before homeroom. Why would I put a note on your locker?"

"Who else in this school goes around making fun of people by turning them into insects?"

"Seriously, it wasn't me," I say. "It's spelled wrong."

"What?"

"It should be 'praying mantis,' with an 'a' because it looks like it's praying." She looks up at the sky as if only God is going to be able to stop her from stepping on me and squishing me into ant-dust. "Honest, Samantha, I didn't write this. I don't even know where your locker is."

She crosses her arms. "Okay, you didn't do it, but it's your work, right? Don't try to pretend you didn't come up with this." I swallow, nod. "And

40

then you told everybody to show them just how smart you were."

I can feel my face burning. "No. I didn't mean it like that, honest, but I'm sorry," I mutter. My voice has gone all dry. I want to scuttle away and hide under a leaf.

She pokes me in the chest again. "You don't even get it, do you?" she says.

"Get what?"

Her shoulders droop as if she's exhausted at the effort of trying to talk to someone so dim. She blows a strand of crinkly hair out of her face. "Maybe you didn't …" Her brow creases, as she tries to find the right words. "Maybe you didn't *throw* the rock but you put it in someone's hand."

It's a pretty good analogy, except that it's aimed right at me. Her face is so angry it looks as if it is cracking around the edges, like there's a bird inside her trying to get out but once the shell opens, there will only be tears.

She snorts with disgust and then turns and strides away.

"'Mantis' comes from the Greek word meaning 'prophet,'" I mutter under my breath.

THERE *IS* a bird in her name, more than one. There's a tern, a magpie, a martin and an ibis. She's almost an egret but needs an extra "e." She's almost a heron but lacks an "o." I google "ibis" when I'm supposed to be doing my math homework and find this great symbolic meaning about an ibis representing a graceful and well-balanced individual. I like that. But I highly doubt Samantha would. Not now. Maybe if I got to know her better and we became friends, I could tell her, secretly, so no one else could hear. I try to imagine whispering it to her. She'd have to bend down a long way to hear or I'd have to stand on a box. If we were friends, I'd probably get a crook in my neck from looking up at her.

MOTH AND I are sitting in homeroom Thursday morning, talking about the new season of *Stranger Things,* when suddenly my name comes on over the intercom.

"Would Anthony Lawson please report to the principal's office?"

Moth looks at me with surprise that is only matched by my own.

I sit outside the principal's office. "Dr. Yasmin Farrokh," it says on the door. I've only ever known her last name until now. Such a beautiful name. Hmm. But before I can find a single creature in it, she's at the door inviting me in.

I sit in front of her desk and she sits behind it. She places her palms together as if she's praying, while looking at something on the desk in front of her. Then she places her hands on the desk, leans forward and looks at me sternly.

"There have been some complaints," she says.

Some complaints? How many is "some"?

"About me?"

She nods then folds her hands on her desktop. "Name-calling is a form of bullying, Anthony," she says. "Do you understand that?"

I nod, swallow hard.

"So what do you have to say for yourself?"

My mouth is dry, my throat tight. I don't know what to say. All I can think is that for someone with such a pretty name it's amazing that there is a mink in her name. Also a shark.

"Anthony?"

"Sorry," I say and try to speak. I can't. I point at my throat.

She reaches into her desk and finds one of those tiny bottles of water and hands it to me. I unscrew the lid, take a long swig, then recap it.

"Thanks," I say.

"You're welcome." She waits. "Well?"

"I just … It's not …" I look down.

"Go on," she says. Her voice is encouraging but a little bit hard, too. The voice of someone who wants an answer, preferably this morning. I take another swig of water.

"I like playing around with words," I say. "That's all it is." I look up at her. She nods vaguely, but if the answer is worth twenty marks on this test, I just got three. "You know, like anagrams and games like that?"

"Like 'astronomer' and 'moon starer,' for example?" she says.

My brain scans the words she just said and I can hardly believe it: they have exactly the same letters, no more, no less. "I never heard that one," I say.

"Playing word games is good for the brain," she says, "and from your school record it seems you have a pretty good brain."

"Thanks," I say.

She only frowns and glances down at her desk top. "But when you start calling people 'Spider-girl' and 'Beavertail' and 'Praying Mantis,' that's a whole other thing."

"I never called anyone those names."

"That's not what I hear."

I shrug and shake my head. "I told Dierdre Prosser she had a spider in her name, and Vera Best she had a beaver in her name, and Samantha Grimsby-Paine she had a praying mantis in her name. That's all. I didn't *call* them that. I swear."

Dr. Farrokh raises a slender black eyebrow. "Then what's this?" she says. She picks up a Post-it Note from her desk and shows it to me.

The Preying Mantis eats guys whole!

I read it and fall back in my seat. "That's … that's …"

"That's what, Anthony?"

"Well, it's spelled wrong for one thing. I told Samantha that yesterday."

"Is that all you've got to say?"

"No. Technically, it's only sort of true. The female mantis doesn't always eat her mate. I mean she does need a lot of protein for making babies, but sometimes she just eats his head. The male is way smaller and —"

"Anthony, I am losing patience here."

"It's just plain nasty," I say. "Is that what you want me to say? Because I agree. Nasty. A hundred percent. Whoever put this on Samantha's locker is a total creep."

"I didn't say it was on her locker," says Dr. Farrokh.

"That's where the other note was stuck. I just assumed …"

"Hmm," she says. "What about this?"

The Beaver sure has a big tail!!!

I shake my head. "That is totally sick."

"'Sick,' how?"

"I don't mean 'sick' as in 'cool.' I mean in the real sense of the word. Someone with muck for brains is doing this."

Dr. Farrokh leans back in her big chair, pulls at one gold earring. I can tell she's running out of patience.

"I didn't do this, Dr. Farrokh."

"Oh, you did," she says.

I freeze at the coldness in her voice. "What do you mean?"

"You're the one who put this out there, correct?

The one who came up with these 'amusing' little word games."

She says "amusing" the way you might say "barf-making."

I shake my head. I wish I was a cockroach instead of an ant. Cockroaches are fast. You swat at them and never get them and then they're back in the woodwork, safe. It takes me time to think. And from the look on the principal's face, my time is running out. I've got to say something. Anything.

"I didn't write those notes, ma'am. I think they're pretty horrible."

Dr. Farrokh leans on her desk and nods again, kind of dismissively. "But the trouble is, you see, you didn't just come up with these creative 'discoveries.' You had to go one step further and brag to your friends about it."

"Whoa! That is so not —"

"Enough. Did you or did you not tell people these nicknames?"

I shake my head. "I told *one* person," I say, holding up a finger. "I told Vera about her name and I told Samantha about hers and I told Dierdre."

Dr. Farrokh's frown deepens. She glances at her elegant gold wristwatch. "Anthony, I don't have time for this."

"It's just that I didn't do it. Somebody else did. And I'm —"

"Stop!" Dr. Farrokh slashes the air with both hands. It's a gesture that means "safe" in baseball, but that's not what it means now. "I've heard quite enough for one day. I'm willing to concede that you *may* not have actually written these disgraceful notes. That said, Mr. Lawson, you broadcast these so-called 'creature names,' and their usage has brought distress to several people. Can you at least accept that this was thoughtless and cruel?"

Thoughtless and cruel.

I stare at Dr. Farrokh. Whatever time there was for discussion is over. I wish I were Rafael Barba from *Law & Order* and could suddenly pull some document from a file and slap it down on her desk — proof positive that it wasn't me, that I wasn't guilty, that I was in another city when the crime took place. I wish I was in another city right now. Maybe another planet.

"Anthony?"

Am I guilty? Did I "broadcast" these creature names? What does that even mean? There may have been other kids around but it's not like I got on the intercom and told the whole school.

"Anthony, I asked you a question, yes or no?"

I stare at her. How do you answer a yes-or-no question when neither option applies? You can't. And I have no words left anyway. All my words have dried up. I know lots and lots of words — I love words! — but they've all gone. I get up and start to leave.

"Excuse me, young man, you have *not* been dismissed!"

I turn to her and swallow hard. "Yes, I have," I say. And leave.

I GO HOME. It's nine in the morning but I was probably going to get kicked out of school anyway. Good. What's the point of school? I'm so angry. I'm so hurt. And at the same time, I feel so guilty for what I did. I *do* get it, Dr. Farrokh: I obviously *did something*. It's just that it isn't what I'm being charged with. Someone else took what I did and did something worse.

Cruel. I hate cruel. *Thoughtless and cruel.*

Am I?

Maybe if I didn't like someone and told them they had something nasty in their name, it would be cruel, but that wasn't what I did. Well, maybe in one case — but I didn't spread it around. And I sure didn't make notes and put them up for other people to see.

I've never felt so many emotions at the same time, whirling around inside me like a tornado, hurling cars and roofs and garbage cans and recliner chairs and little dogs around inside my head until I'm exhausted and I sit down on my bed, empty.

And what do I end up with? Stupid, that's what.

Stupid and embarrassed. Embarrassed that someone — anyone — thinks I'm a bad person. Embarrassed to have hurt someone's feelings. Especially someone I admire, like Samantha. Mostly I'm sad. Deep-down-in-my-bones sad. I'm just the little twit who plays around with words and thinks he's a big deal, like he discovered the source of the Nile or how to split the atom.

MOTH TEXTS me at lunch.

Dude?

I'm in jail. Bring me Miss Vickie's.

Harvest Cheddar, right?

Sí.

You got it, mi amigo.

He comes over after school. He already knows what happened, or at least some of it. A lot of people think I was kicked out of school. I couldn't care less. But that's not true. I do care and I hate caring.

"I don't like her," says Moth.

"Who? Samantha?" He nods. "Do you think she did this?"

He nods again. "She thinks she's this crusader for justice but she's *una bravucona*. That's all. A bully."

I want to agree with him but I can't. "She didn't tell on me," I say. "At least, I don't think so."

"Then who?"

"It doesn't matter," I say. The last thing I want to do right now is accuse someone without any proof.

"You're a good person," he says, patting me on the shoulder. "You suck at *Monster Hunter* but you're a good person."

"Thanks," I say, even though I feel like I don't deserve it.

"Hey," he says, "don't forget who you are. You are the mighty Ant, able to carry burdens one hundred times your body weight." We bump fists. I don't tell him that right now I can barely lift my own leg. I don't want to go anywhere. Ever.

—

"Is THIS someone you know?" says Mom. She's watching the six-o'clock news in the kitchen while she makes dinner. There's some kind of march on Parliament Hill. Teenagers mostly, but children, too, carrying signs and chanting. But in the foreground, there's Samantha! She's holding a sign that reads, "ACT NOW OR SWIM LATER." The local station is interviewing her.

"That's why it's called FridaysForFuture," she's saying. She smiles defiantly. Behind her I read the other signs. It's all about climate change and saving the planet.

Then the picture changes to kids marching in the UK, Belgium, Germany, Switzerland and Sweden. The camera zooms in on a pack of people in Stockholm. In the center there's a girl holding a sign in Swedish. She's sixteen but looks quite little, like me. Her name is Greta. Greta Thunberg. She's the one who started this whole thing. I've never heard a thing about it.

"It's sometimes annoying," says Greta, "when people say, 'Oh, you children, you young people are the hope. You will save the world.' I think it would be helpful if you could help just a little."

"Right on, Greta!" I say. "Wow!"

Then the camera returns to the talking head in

the newsroom, who is smiling as if what she said was cute. Then he gets serious again. There's another scandal: some government official has been caught accepting bribes.

"Some kids will use any excuse to get out of school," says my mother, giving me the stink eye. Thanks, Mom.

I head back to my room and look up Greta Thunberg and FridaysForFuture. All over the world, kids are going on strike every Friday to march for the sake of the Earth and the climate. The prime minister of England says they're wasting lesson time. And what does Greta tweet back? "That may well be the case. But then again, political leaders have wasted 30 yrs of inaction. And that is slightly worse."

"Woo-hoo!" I shout to my empty room. I love the way she says "slightly worse." Because you just have to say, no wait — it's WAY worse.

"Who are you talking to?" Mom shouts upstairs.

"No one," I shout back down.

"It's dinner," she says.

But I just keep reading. She calls me again. But I'm hooked on what I'm finding. By the time I finally do go downstairs, kind of dazed, she and Dad are watching TV in the living room, something with lots of squealing tires and gunshots. My dinner awaits me on the counter, ready to nuke: mashed potatoes, beans and a sweaty porkchop. I stare at it, my mind on fire.

I MISS Friday but my mom talks to Principal Farrokh and I'm allowed to come back Monday as long as I don't do any more name-calling. Mom and Dad are shocked by my behavior. I start to explain, but only kind of half-heartedly. They aren't listening anyway.

I'm grounded for the weekend. Do a lot more reading about climate change and get angrier and angrier. Ninety-seven percent of scientists agree that global warming is a reality and yet there are all these people who deny, deny, deny. I'm not sure who's worse — the ones who pretend it isn't happening or the ones who believe in it and still don't do anything. All I can say is that climate change is definitely happening in my bedroom. I'm getting very, very hot under the collar.

MONDAY, first thing, I go looking for Samantha, wandering the halls until I find her locker. I know it's hers because she's there. Her locker door has a picture of a polar bear sitting in an ice cream cone.

The polar bear is melting.

"What do you want?" she says, looking at me as if maybe I'm carrying a concealed weapon.

"I saw you on TV," I say.

"So? Do you want an autograph?"

I shake my head. "I was pretty impressed."

She doesn't speak right away, as if she's expecting a trick. Then she seems to reach some kind of conclusion. She turns and reaches into her locker. She pulls out a clipboard and hands it to me, shoves a pen in my hand.

"Okay, if you were so impressed, why not sign this petition?"

I take the clipboard and read what it says. It's a letter to the school board asking them to make Earth Day — April 22nd — a day to celebrate and encourage global awareness. There's going to be a big rally in the capital and Samantha wants the school to lay on buses so students can join the protest. She's only got about five names.

"You'd think everybody would want to get a day off school," I say, adding my name, address and phone number to the petition.

"It's not about skipping school," she says, her voice peevish. "It's about *doing* something. Making a diff —"

"I know, I know!" I slam the pen down on her clipboard. "I was grounded all weekend — you can guess why — and do you want to know what I did?"

"Not really."

"Good, then I'll tell you. I read all about Greta Thunberg and FridaysForFuture. That's what I did. And then I read a whole lot more on climate change."

For a moment she seems to really see me, but she quickly reverts to surly. "Well, good for you. Do you want a medal?"

I shake my head. "No," I say. "I felt stupid not knowing about it. I mean, I knew but I didn't know enough. And when I don't know about something, I look it up. I may be stupid but I'm not as stupid as you think."

"Knowing isn't doing," she says.

"It's a start," I say.

She frowns and shrugs. Then she takes out the books she needs for the morning, piles them on her clipboard and closes her locker. She looks down at me — she can't help it, I'm so short.

"For the record, I never said you were stupid."

"No, just kind of a waste of time," I say.

"I didn't say that, either."

"I know, but you think it."

She shakes her head. "I think you do *waste* your time, yes. I don't think you *are* a waste of time."

"You think the world needs saving. Good. I agree. And I want to do something about it." She glares at me. "I'm not kidding. I'm not just saying it."

"Did the principal put you up to this?"

I shake my head but now I'm as peeved as she is and too angry, all over again, to say anything. I walk away.

"Anthony!" she says. I turn. She gestures me to come closer. "You're only mad because someone wrote those stupid notes and you got blamed for it. You're mad because someone blabbed on you to Farrokh. You just don't want to accept any blame at all."

"That's not —"

"Let me finish," she says. "I don't know if you've figured it out yet but FridaysForFuture is all about accountability. Politicians talk, talk, talk and do nothing. Ever. Half the time the words aren't even theirs. They've got fancy speech writers who use words to smother the truth."

"I know, but —"

"Which is why I get pissed off when I run into someone who's really, really good at words but who doesn't seem to care one thing about what those words are saying — what they're doing."

Her eyebrows rise like they're asking me a question: Are you that kind of person?

It's a challenge. One I can't answer. I'm struck speechless.

I PASS HER in the hall later, and the question is still there. I keep walking. At lunch, I avoid her and her eyes. I thought I was done being angry and embarrassed and hurt. And sad. I'm not done. Not nearly.

Which is why I get pissed off when I run into someone who's really, really good at words but who doesn't seem to care one thing about what those words are saying — what they're doing.

Is that me? I don't know, but suddenly I don't trust myself to speak. Don't trust words anymore. I'll stop talking. Nobody will ever be able to accuse me of being thoughtless and cruel. Nobody will ever accuse me of putting rocks in anybody's hand. I'll become invisible. An ant meandering from one place to another, not carrying a thing.

THE NEXT morning, she's at my locker. Samantha. She's leaning against it, holding her clipboard to her chest. I wonder if there's a way that the sentence, "Could you please move so that I could get to my locker?" could be taken as cruel and thoughtless?

Luckily, I don't have to speak; she moves aside. But as I start turning my combination, she holds the petition out for me to see. She's got pages and pages — fifty names in all. I give her two thumbs up and open my locker door. Then she points at one name. Dierdre Prosser. I look at the way Dierdre printed her name with the *e*'s kind of open like *c*'s; just like the *e* in "preying mantis" in the note that was on Samantha's locker and the *e* in "beaver" in the notes on Dr. Farrokh's desk.

"Whoa," I say. I want to be angry, but how can I be when Samantha went to the trouble of proving it wasn't me?!

"Did you think I went to the principal?" she asks outright.

"No," I say. "I'd kind of guessed it was her."

"Because that isn't the way I roll," she says. "If I have something to say to someone, I say it. I don't go blabbing to the authorities. You get it?" I nod. "I don't have much patience with the authorities," she says.

That I can believe.

"So, what's up with you? Cat got your tongue?"

I look at her and all I can think to say is, "I'm not a bad person."

She nods. "Good. Now can you get over yourself?"

"What I did was, like, an inadvertent bad thing. Dierdre goes out of her way to do bad things. It makes me so angry."

"Yeah, yeah, yeah. I do lots of things — on purpose — that really get under people's skin because lots of people are complacent and smug and self-satisfied and if anyone says stuff that reminds them of what they don't want to think about, they get angry. They're not angry at me, I tell myself. They're angry at themselves, even though it sure *feels* as if they're angry at me. But it's worth it, you know, if I'm getting the message out there."

"Is there a point you're trying to make?"

"Yes!" she says. "You can't waste your time moping around because people don't like you or think you're someone you're not. In fact, the more I stir people up, the more I know I'm getting something done. Do you get that?"

I don't know what to say. I think maybe it's the bravest thing I ever heard. I nod.

"Don't be dumb," she says.

"Hey!"

She rolls her eyes. "I didn't mean it like that. I meant don't get all silent and hurt. You've got words, use them. But use them for a reason, okay? Use them to fight back."

"Yeah," I say, although I am still dumbstruck.

"So, are you ready for action?" she says.

I slam my locker door. It's a cliché, I know, but there it was hanging open in front of me and something had to be done.

"You're angry," she says. "Angry is good." Then she looks around. My locker door slam got people glancing our way. Samantha moves in close enough to whisper. "You want to get angry at something way more important than some sneaky mean girl?"

"Yes," I say. It sounds better than "yeah," like I really mean it. It's just one word — one syllable — but it sounds good coming from my mouth. So good I say it again. "Yes."

Her face brightens just a bit. "You'd better mean it, because this is really important. Adults think we're just going to drop the whole thing. They don't know how serious we are."

"*That* you didn't need to tell me."

"And what about you? Are you serious?"

"I think so. I mean, I get it, but …"

"But what, Anthony?"

Don't call me that, I want to say to her — shout at her. I'm just an ant. I'm so small and insignificant. I can't do this!

"Are you okay?"

I shake my head. Who am I kidding? Even if I can carry a hundred times my weight, that's hardly anything when you look at the big picture.

"Anthony?"

"I'm afraid," I say and flinch like she's going to yell at me. But instead her face softens a bit — not so much granite anymore but soapstone.

"Do you ever get called names?" she says. I stare at her. "Because I sure do. Stretch, Skyscraper, Spaghetti Legs."

I grin. "Trade you for Mini-Me, Peanut, Squirt."

"Statue of Liberty, Sky High?"

"How about Shrimp, Small Stuff, Ankle Biter?" We both laugh. "Sky High's not too bad," I say. "As in 'the sky's the limit.'"

Then there is silence between us. Which is interesting, considering it's just a few minutes before the bell, and the whole school seems to have gone dead quiet. Maybe it's the end of the world and all the oxygen has been sucked right out of it so there's nothing left to hear, no birds singing, no creatures stirring, not even a mouse. Still, I hear her just fine when she speaks again.

"I'm afraid, too," she says.

I stare at her. "Really?"

"Yeah. But I can't let that stop me. This might be the last chance we have. I mean, politicians are all about winning elections and what the polls say. They don't *do* anything. We can't wait around. It's now or never. You know?" I nod but I guess she senses my hesitancy. "You've got to, got to, *got to* care."

I look down, give my neck a break. All I can think of is that I'm twelve and suddenly I'm supposed to drop everything and help save the world because adults can't be bothered. Then I look up again and see this hope in her face and I know, somehow, that she's right and it's got to happen.

"I do care," I say. "I'm caring the best I can."

Then she smiles. It's the first smile I've ever seen on her. "You want to march this Friday?"

I swallow hard. Nod. Then nod again. Vigorously.

"Good," she says. "Let's do it." She looks away and then does a double take. "It's not a date, okay. Got that?"

"As if," I say.

"Maybe you can come up with some clever slogans."

I nod. "Yeah, sure. I wonder what Greta Thunberg's creature name is?"

"Don't you —"

"Kidding!" I say. "But here's something, anyway: 'Greta is Great.'" I print it in the sky as if they're words on a poster.

"You're right," she says. "My hero."

"Thanks."

"Not you, her. Oh, wait!" Her eyes light up. Good, she finally got it.

"There's all kinds of things hidden in a person's name," I say.

Then we just look at each other. It's silent but not because the world has ended, simply because the bell rang some time ago now, and we're the only ones left in the hall.

"Friday," she says.

I salute. She rolls her eyes and starts off down the hall.

"I'm not sure I'll be able to keep up with you," I call after her.

She swings around. "No long-legged jokes, please," she says.

Ant and the Praying Mantis

"Okay," I say and cross my heart. Truth is I'm really not sure I'll be able to keep up with her. But I'm going to try.

THE PLEDGE

"DINNER TIME," I said through the door of my dad's office.

No response.

"It's meat loaf," I said.

"I thought we were having chicken."

"Nope," I said and turned to go.

"I've been looking forward to roast chicken all day," he called after me.

I stopped. Would I tell him? I wanted to like crazy, but it was Mom's story. "There's a good reason for no chicken," I said.

—

"WHERE'S DAD?" said Randy, helping himself to meat loaf and baby potatoes and creamed corn and ketchup and bread and butter and pickles.

"Dead," I said.

"Can I have his meat loaf, Mom?"

Mom made that irritated tsking noise and started feeding the baby, who didn't want mashed potato and carrot and whatever other mashed up things she had in her bowl. She pointed at Randy's plate and said, "Dat, dat, dat!" until Mom airplaned a spoonful of mush into her mouth to shut her up.

Dad finally joined us, tapping the top of his wristwatch.

"I know, I know," said Mom. "You're dying of hunger. It couldn't be helped."

Dad sat and looked glumly at the table as if there were an open casket there and his dearest friend was lying in it.

"What happened to the roast chicken?" he said.

Mom stopped feeding the baby, got up and plopped portions of everything on a plate for Dad.

"This morning you promised me roast chicken with stuffing and gravy and all the trimmings."

Mom came around the table and banged the plate down in front of Dad with such force that one of the potatoes escaped, bounced and rolled under the table, where Ginger barked at it.

"There was a robbery at the grocery store," said Mom.

"A what?"

"Ginger, out from there. Out!" said Mom.

My four-year-old sister crawled out from under the table, the runaway potato in her mouth, and climbed into her seat. She was going through a phase of thinking she was a dog.

Dad looked at his plate and shook his head. "Did they take all the chicken?"

"Oh, for goodness' sakes," said Mom, feeding Belinda, or trying to.

"It's true," I said. "That's why Mom was late and we don't have chicken. She was a witness and had to talk to a detective and everything."

"Don't talk with your mouth full," said Mom.

"At Safeway?" said Dad.

"Doesn't sound all that safe," said Randy. "More like Dangerway."

"It wasn't all that much of a business," said Mom.

Then Baby Belinda brought her hand down — SMOOSH! — right in the middle of her bowl and wiped the smile right off Mom's face. Well, not really. It was just that mashed food covered it up. The smile, I mean.

"Tell us, Mom," I said. I had learned only so much when she got home, before she shooed me out of the kitchen.

She sat back and sighed. She looked around the table, and we were all staring back at her, except for Belinda, who was all hands in and having a great time, splattering potato and who knows what every which way. Even Ginger stopped licking her plate to look up.

"Were you in any danger?" said Dad.

Mom finished wiping the mush from her face with her napkin and managed a fragile little smile. "Not really. The robber was in line ahead of me at the cashier."

"Holy crap!" said Randy.

"Yap, yap, yap," said Ginger enthusiastically. I patted her on the head.

"He pulled out a gun once the —"

"He what?" said Dad and Randy and me all together. Ginger whimpered. Belinda just laughed. Her face was barely visible through the food encrusted there.

Mom threw down her napkin. "Would you please let me finish?" she said. She stared at her plate, as if she was sorry for the all the work she'd put into making a dinner that nobody was going to get around to eating. "He pulled out a gun once all his groceries were packed up and said he wasn't going to pay for them because he didn't have any money. Or something like that. Then he walked out."

"Whoa!" I said.

"I'm not sure it was a real gun," said Mom.

"How do you know?" said Randy.

"Well, I don't," said Mom, suddenly frowning.

"But they were real groceries?" said Dad.

"The poor cashier fainted," said Mom.

"Then I guess they were real groceries," said Dad.

"I don't think anyone else noticed what was going on. It was busy. There was the usual hubbub — you know — and he was very soft-spoken. For a robber. Not that I've ever encountered a robber before."

"So you were the only one who saw him?" I said breathlessly.

"Apart from the cashier," said Randy. "But did she, like, hit her head on the counter as she fell and couldn't remember anything when she recovered, not even her name or where she lives, so that you were the only witness?"

Mom frowned again. "It was Agnes," she said. "You know, the one with the big mole. And she knew perfectly well who *she* was. She just didn't know who the robber was."

"Did you?" said Dad.

Mom shook her head. "He was wearing a long coat in very bad repair. Gabardine. Honey-colored. I'd been looking at the hem while I waited for him to place his things on the conveyor belt. I thought someone should fix that coat. It was old but had a lot of good wear left in it. A Burberry, if I'm not mistaken."

"Burglary?" said Dad. "That's when you enter a building with intent to commit a theft."

"*Burberry,*" said Mom again. "His coat. Must have got it at the Sally Ann."

"So was he, like, a street person?" said Randy. "Was he all grotty and unshaved, with crud down the front of his coat and, like, boots with holes in them and no laces?"

"Oh, for goodness' sakes, Randy," said Mom, shaking her head in despair. "What a dreadful, dreadful generalization."

"So, what did he look like?" I asked.

"Well, he was wearing a red hat."

"Aha!" said Randy. "A Canadiens fan. A lot of street people are Canadiens fans." We all stared at Randy. "It's true," he said. Then, when we didn't stop staring, he shrugged and went back to eating his dinner.

"It wasn't a hockey toque," said Mom. "And it wasn't meant to be red. It had been white at one time, but it was filthy and had a big red smear across the top of it."

I had started eating again, but now I put down my fork and stared at my plate.

"Hmm," said Dad. "You can bet that hat won't surface again. Probably dropped it in the nearest dumpster."

"Did you see the getaway car?" said Randy.

"He doesn't have a car," I said.

"How would you know?" said Randy.

I didn't answer.

"What is it, Joseph?" said Mom.

I didn't answer. And then I said, "Can I call Danny?"

I wasn't allowed to call until we'd eaten and helped to clean up.

"We've got to talk," I said.

"I'll be right over," said Danny.

We sat out back at the picnic table. I didn't want anyone to overhear us.

"It's about Mr. Gower," I said.

"Oh, no," said Danny. "Why now? It was so long ago! Did he go to the cops? I told you he saw us. He saw us, right? I knew it, I knew it."

I waited for Danny to finish. He's very anxious and you can't really interrupt him when he's having one of his panic attacks, even if what you've got to say would relieve him of his anxiety.

"It was so stupid," he said, rubbing his hands together. "We were so stupid. Why did we do it, Joe? It's not like he'd ever done anything to us."

I waited and watched him squirm. I looked up and saw Mom at the kitchen window watching us. Sometimes Danny gets pretty loud when he's freaking out. I waved and she turned away.

Danny took a deep breath and squeezed his eyes shut. "Tell me," he said, as if I was a judge and he was only wondering whether he was getting Life or the Electric Chair.

"He robbed a grocery store," I said.

Danny's eyes opened. He stared at me with this confused expression on his face as if I'd completely changed the topic of conversation. "He what?"

The Pledge

So I told him Mom's story, and when I got to the red hat, he gasped.

"Oh," he said.

"Right."

His forehead wrinkled, as if he was forty or something — real old. "So what do we do?"

I wasn't sure. I had a kind of a plan but I didn't know if Danny's anxiety disorder could handle it. Then again, we had a deal. We'd made a pledge. I wasn't about to do it alone and nobody else could help. The big question was whether we'd keep our promise to each other. Me and Danny.

OUT PAST the train tracks that run behind the mall, out where the county road scoots out of town to the southwest, just past the place where the old people live and the veterinary clinic where doctors look after *real* dogs, not imaginative four-year-old girls, there's a rusted and overgrown Quonset hut. It's the only thing that's left of the once-upon-a-time stockyards, and out past that, there's a rundown old farm that nobody lives on. Dad once told me the land was probably valuable, that eventually Ladybank would expand out that way and whoever was sitting on that property would make a pretty penny.

I told Danny about it. We told each other every-thing back then — still do. And then, one Saturday when Danny wasn't feeling too anxious, we decided to go looking for this patient person who'd been sitting on the land, waiting so long for Ladybank to grow. Which is when we discovered Mr. Gower.

"Is that him?" Danny whispered.

"I don't know," I said. "He isn't sitting."

"Well, he couldn't sit all the time," said Danny. "It's just an expression."

Mr. Gower was walking when we saw him, walking along what had probably once been a road — the driveway — leading up to the fall-down farm. The grass was almost as high as he was and higher than we were, but we'd taken up a position in a tall maple and Danny had brought his father's binoculars.

"He looks just like that guy in the movie," Danny said.

"That narrows it down," I said.

"You know. The Christmas movie. The one where the kid goes through the ice and there's an angel trying to earn his wings and a banker and —"

"*It's a Wonderful Life?*"

Danny nodded, and I took the binoculars from him.

"The drugstore guy," he said. "The one who almost poisons someone by mistake."

"Mr. Gower," I said, pulling the old man in on the binoculars.

But what Danny meant was this guy looked like the bad Mr. Gower, the one who had become a drunk after he'd gone to prison for poisoning the guy, because there was no young George Bailey to stop him. That was how he looked, all right. A moment later he walked right under the tree where we were perched. He didn't see us, didn't look up. He was singing a song, but you couldn't make out the words.

Cats started appearing out of the high grass. They must have heard him singing and followed him down the road toward the farmhouse. Bunches of them.

WE WERE about nine, then, Danny and me. It didn't take us long to realize Mr. Gower didn't own the farm and he wasn't expecting to make a million dollars anytime soon. He wasn't "sitting" on the land, he was squatting, living there illegally — but nobody seemed to know, except us. You'd see him around town sometimes. He had an old bike with a box on the back of it. Sometimes there'd be stuff in the box, mostly junk. We'd never seen him in the honey-colored coat my mom described, the one he was wearing when he robbed the store, but we knew the hat, all right. Danny and I were the reason his white hat was splotchy red on top.

We'd just learned about water balloons.

I'm not sure how we got it into our heads to drop one on Mr. Gower. I guess it was because he was an easy target. By then we had spied on him a fair bit. We'd climb up that big old maple beside the once-upon-a-time driveway and he'd come by on his bike or on foot. He'd sing and cats would appear and march down the road like it was a parade and he was the not-so-grand marshal. By then, we'd made up a lot of stories about Mr. Gower.

Anyway, it was summer and we had nothing to do and we biked over to his place and were up in his tree and we had these water balloons filled with Club House red food coloring. It just sort of happened. There he was, walking up the overgrown road and even though it was summer he had on an old black raincoat and a white toque and … well …

Splash!
Splash!

He stopped. He was standing directly below us. One balloon missed but the other hit him on the top of his head — a direct hit. *Splat!* We clung to our branch, Danny and me, not breathing. Trying to look as small as we felt. We waited, too scared to move.

What if Mr. Gower ate children? If he was wanted by the FBI, maybe it was because he was a serial killer. If he was in hiding from the mob, maybe he'd been their hit man. We waited and Mr. Gower just stood there, dripping. He never looked up. The dye soaked into his white hat, bright red, as if we had broken open his skull and blood was pouring out. And he never looked up. Maybe getting hit on the head by things falling from the sky was something that had happened to him before. Maybe he was used to it. Maybe it was something falling from the sky that had made him like he was.

The cats skedaddled when the bombs dropped. And after about a hundred hours, Mr. Gower moved on, as well, and stared singing the song he'd been singing when the sky broke open above him and gave him a blood-red soaker.

———

IT WAS BACK at Danny's that we made the pledge. Danny's anxiety was working overtime.

"What were we thinking!?" he said.

"We weren't."

"It's just an expression," he said.

"I know."

"But what *were* we thinking, Joe!?"

I didn't say anything for a moment, just stared at my friend and tried to imagine what was going on inside his head. I had to do something.

"I've got it!" I said. Danny stared at me, his eyes like saucers, but with some hope spilling into the worry there. "We can't take back what we did, right?"

Danny shook his head.

"But we can make a promise," I said.

"To who? To him?"

"Uh, no. To each other."

"What good's that going to do?"

"We could, you know, help him."

"How? Pay for a dry cleaner?"

"No. I mean if he needs help sometime."

"Are you kidding? He needs help all the time. He's loony. He's a crazy person. He lives in a fall-down house. He rides a bike with pink streamers on the handlebars. He —"

The Pledge

"I know, I know," I said, cutting him off before he went full tilt. "Take a deep breath," I said.

He did. In and then out. Then he shook his arms and ran on the spot and did a kind of shortened version of the Hokey Pokey. "Okay," he said at last. "You said something about a promise?"

I nodded. "A pledge," I said. The word had come to me while I'd been watching him try to slow down his runaway nerves. Pledge sounded more serious. Like something worthy.

"What we did was stupid. We can't take it back but we can keep tabs on Mr. Gower and if he ever needs help, we can try to … I don't know … do something. Do something right."

It didn't sound very convincing, but somehow Danny got it. We agreed. We shook on it. It was a relief. We'd done a dumb thing and were going to pay for it. Just not now. Sometime. Some unspecified time.

And then we forgot all about it.

WE WERE nine back then. What did we know?

Anyway, we hadn't spied on the abandoned farmhouse for years. Now, we were twelve. And yet here he was again, Mr. Gower, back in our life. Mr. Gower, who clearly needed help.

And here were Danny and I, who had made a pledge.

It was getting dark. Mom was at the kitchen window again, looking out at us, wondering what we were up to. *It's okay, Mom. We're just going to help out an old crazy person who is obviously in some kind of big trouble, because we have to, because we made a pledge.*

"Even if he has a gun?" said Danny.

"We'll be careful," I said. "We'll tackle him outside."

"Tackle him?"

"I mean, you know, approach him ... carefully."

I'm not sure if Danny heard me or not; he was thinking about that gun. I could see it in his eyes.

It wasn't hard to get together a whole lot of groceries. Mom always filled the cupboard with lots of tinned stuff and boxes of mac and cheese, in case there was another ice storm or a zombie apocalypse or whatever. She wouldn't miss what we took. The same was true for Danny's mother. She was even more generous because Danny told her it was a food drive. It wasn't so big a lie, really. If Mr. Gower was hungry enough to hold up a grocery store, then he was just as needy as anyone who used the food bank.

This was our plan. We'd take him a whole bunch of food — two cardboard boxes full. And then we'd tell him about the food bank. We'd take him there, if he didn't know where it was. I'd helped out there with my parents at Christmas, so I knew where it was and how nice the people were who worked there.

"And then we're done, right?" said Danny.

"The pledge?"

He nodded. "Does a couple of boxes of food make up for a water bomb on the head?"

I gave it some serious thought. Then I nodded. "A box for each bomb," I said.

"Even though mine missed him?" said Danny.

"It was mine that missed him," I said.

But we'd been through all this back when it happened. We had decided we were both guilty. It just felt better if we both thought we'd missed.

So, on Saturday, we strapped the boxes onto the carriers of our bikes and headed out of town to the abandoned farm, where only we knew that Mr. Gower lived. I don't think we'd ever known the county road was uphill until that day. It was hard work. The boxes weighed us down something awful. But we made it, and stopped, out of breath, at the end of the drive.

There was a mailbox at the entranceway. The door was gone and there looked to be a nest inside.

"We should make some noise," I said as we approached the house.

"No way!" said Danny. "That will give him time to load up."

"I meant nice noise. We could sing," I said, "like he does."

"Yeah, and get attacked by all those cats!"

Danny wagged his head so hard he almost lost his balance. It was hard enough riding through the undergrowth that had reclaimed the driveway. "We've got to take him by surprise," he said. "Give him the groceries and get out of there. Done."

"Okay," I said quietly, not wanting to rile him up any more than he was. We'd talked about all of this.

"Leave the groceries by the gate, right? Get his attention, show him the boxes and then take off."

I wasn't going to argue. The closer we got, the more nervous I got. Maybe I'd been hanging out with Danny too long.

The Pledge

We stopped at the broken-down fence that surrounded the broken-down house. We leaned our bikes against the rusted gate post and hefted the boxes of food off the back of our bikes.

"Carry it like this," said Danny really quietly. He had the box right in front of him. "That way if he shoots, he'll only hit a can of beans or something."

"Okay," I said, and shivered at the thought of all that bean juice dripping on the ground like blood.

I entered the gate. The pathway to the house must have been rolled up by the people who last lived there and taken with them to wherever it was they moved. There was just a trail through the high grass, the kind of trail deer make in the forest, only as wide as they are. His bike was on the porch. So were cats. Two or three anyway. Then I saw a couple in the yard. One on the fence. Another watching from the drooping porch roof.

I was so busy cat-spotting I didn't realize I was alone. I stopped and turned. Danny was still standing at the gateway. He hadn't moved. I went back.

"I thought we were just going to leave the boxes," he whispered.

"Sorry," I said. "I forgot. But, you know, it's broad daylight. I don't think he'd do anything, as long as we told him we were bringing him stuff."

"Don't you think we should have just told the food bank people about him and let them do this?" he whispered.

I looked at him. I didn't want to admit I was on the verge of chickening out, too. I mean, we were nine when we made the pledge, right? We were just kids. Stupid kids. We didn't write it down or anything. We didn't sign our names in blood. Nobody would know what we did and nobody would know we backed out of it. Nobody but us.

I didn't say anything. I just locked eyes with Danny. If he couldn't do it, with his anxiety thing and all, then what was I supposed to do? Stand by him, my best friend? Or stand by this promise we made each other? Then as I looked at him his eyes grew wide and I realized he wasn't looking at me anymore, he was looking past me.

"Uh-oh," he murmured.

I slowly turned and there was Mr. Gower, standing on his porch looking straight at us. He was wearing a ragged check sports jacket over a mustard-yellow T-shirt and bib overalls. The good news was that he wasn't pointing a gun at us. The bad news was that he was carrying an axe.

"If them are kittens, you can just take them back where you come from," he said.

It wasn't what I had expected him to say. "Pardon?" I said.

"People keep leaving kittens. They don't want them so they just leave 'em here. Boxes and boxes of 'em. I can't barely keep up."

Oh.

"They're not kittens," I said.

"Are they puppies? I don't like puppies."

I cleared my throat. "They're not kittens," I said more loudly. "Or dogs."

He nodded slowly as if he only half-believed me. "So, is it cat food, maybe?" he asked. "That would sure come in handy."

"No, sir," I said.

"It's people food," said Danny.

I looked at him. He'd come out of his stupor. He hoisted the box higher, so that it was covering his heart, just in case. He looked at me and bravely started walking up the path that wasn't there. I wasn't so sure if a cardboard box of canned foods would be a good defense against an axe, but I was impressed with Danny. I followed after him.

It was only then that I wished we'd told anyone where we were going.

"People food?" Mr. Gower said when we arrived at his stoop. He was only a step higher up than us, but he was pretty tall and gangly. He leaned his axe against a post that was already leaning all by itself — only just barely holding up the porch roof. He peeked in Danny's box. He frowned. Then he peeked in mine, frowned some more. He reached in and took out a fat can of cabbage rolls and really frowned. Then he put it back.

"Is this for me?" he said.

We nodded. Then I said, "Yes, sir."

He nodded again and then scratched his head. "Is this a school project?" he asked.

"No, sir," I said.

"I don't want to be no school project," he said.

"It's just from us," said Danny.

"Never much liked teachers," he said.

"We figured you might like some food," I said.

Mr. Gower looked truly perplexed. "It ain't Christmas for three months," he said.

He was wrong about that. It wasn't Christmas for seven months. But the box was getting heavy. We needed to move this thing along. "It isn't a

Christmas present," I said. "We just thought you were, you know, really hungry."

"On account of robbing the grocery store," said Danny.

He just said it like that, out of the blue. I stared at him and then glanced at Mr. Gower to see if he was going to pick up his axe or reach into the pocket of his grotty old jacket for his gun.

But he wasn't. He was nodding his head. "Oh, that," he said. "That was an accident."

Danny looked at me and I looked at him.

"An accident?"

"Yeah, yeah, yeah," he said. Then he scratched his head again and chuckled. "Woo-ee," he said and then he stared across the overgrown lawn with a smile on his face.

"Sir, could we put this stuff down?" I said.

He looked down at us, squinting, as if in the moment he'd looked away, he'd totally forgotten we were there.

"Oh, sure. Sure. Whyn't you bring it in here." He turned toward the door, opened it and stood aside, like a doorman, to let us pass.

We were met by cats. There must have been an-other dozen of them in the kitchen. We had to sort of shove them out of the way with our feet in order to reach the table, where we put down the boxes and breathed a sigh of relief. Two sighs of relief, one each.

"Now what's all this about?" he asked.

"We heard about what happened," I said. "And we sort of knew it was you."

"You did?"

"Yes, sir, on account of your hat," I said. He reached up, feeling for a hat. "The one you were wearing that day. The white toque with the big red stain."

"We knew that hat," said Danny, jumping in. I thought he'd say more but he clammed up.

I think maybe we'd overloaded Mr. Gower's motherboard. His frown deepened as if he was having to think long and hard to grasp what we were saying. And then, all of a sudden, his face cleared up and he just sort of stared at nothing — nothing we could see.

"Well, thank you boys for the food," he said. "I never turn down food." He looked at us and then he got up and walked over to a big old kitchen cabinet and opened the doors. It was full of food.

"But ... But ..."

"It's okay, Danny," I said.

"Yeah, but —"

"We'll be going now," I said, grabbing Danny's shoulder.

"You robbed a grocery store," said Danny.

I groaned.

Mr. Gower shrugged his shoulders. "Yep," he said. "I did. But like I said it was an accident. I didn't mean to."

"You … you pulled a gun," said Danny.

"Danny," I whisper-shouted, dragging my hand across my throat.

Mr. Gower laughed and then scratched his hair. Things fell out as he did. I didn't look too closely.

"Well, you see, I'd been to see Evening Primrose. You'll know her," he said. Danny was just about to say something like, *We have no idea what you are talking about*, but I elbowed him to shut up. "She'd been sickly and I dropped in to see if there was anything I could do. You know, run an errand for her. She gave me some money to go get her a few things. So I did."

He stopped as if he'd explained the whole thing. End of story. His smile faded a little bit and he looked off across the kitchen. It was pretty tidy, really, if you didn't count all the cats. I sniffed. It didn't even smell as bad as you'd think. Then Mr.

Gower's eyes found us again, saw us standing there and he startled, as if it was taking him a moment or two to remember who we were or why we were there.

"Oh, right," he said. "The gun." Then he started poking around in his pocket. "I've got it here somewhere —"

"That's okay," I said.

"Oh, wait," he said. "No, I don't. I gave it back to Cyrus. Cyrus or Bob. Not sure which. One of Primrose's boys. You know Cyrus and Bob?" he asked. We shook our heads. "No, I guess not. They're just little 'uns, five or six … something like that."

Danny looked at me out of the corner of his eye.

Then Mr. Gower put his big old hands on his knees and leaned forward, chuckling away.

"I remember it now. There I was in the check-out line with Primrose's groceries and when I was feeling in my pocket for the money she'd gived me, instead, I find this thing in my pocket. I pull it out and it's this old-fashioned six-shooter. Plastic. I guess one of her kids put it in my pocket — who knows why? Kids," he said and shook his head as if he'd never be able to figure them out.

"So I show the girl, you know — the one be-hind the counter. And I says to her, 'Look at this, will ya. Guess you'll have to give me these here groceries for free.'"

He burst out laughing and smacked his knee with his hand. "Next thing I know, she'd gone. Didn't see her leave or nothing. I looked behind me, saw there was a line-up, so I just … you know … left." He smiled at us. Chuckled a bit. "Now, that's not the place I usually shop, you see. It just happens to be right nearby Primrose's place. But hey, if they're givin' away groceries, maybe I should go there more often."

WE SAID our goodbyes and Mr. Gower thanked us again for the food. And we were heading up the path that was just a bit wider than when we arrived on account of Danny and me walking side by side, when suddenly my best friend turned around and headed back toward the house. The door was still open, but he knocked on it any-way, and Mr. Gower turned to see who it was. He was standing at the counter opening a can of cat food with a herd of cats at his feet. He glow-ered at us. "I hope you didn't bring me no more cats," he said.

Danny cleared his throat. "We dropped a wa-ter balloon filled with red food coloring on your head," he said. "About three years ago. We're sorry we did it."

Mr. Gower showed no signs of having under-stood what Danny said. I wasn't entirely sure he recognized us, to tell the truth.

Then Danny turned and headed back up the path. I waved goodbye to Mr. Gower and followed him. We ran, grabbed our bikes, and headed up the driveway. We flew. Fast as lightning. The bikes were so much lighter without the weight we'd come there carrying.

THE JOURNEY TO OMPAH

My Dad is so polite his pants catch on fire. Okay, just the once. And it was the bird's fault, a bird that had no business being in this part of the world. Then again, you have to wonder … If it hadn't been for the bird and the cute reporter and the burning trousers …

But let me start at the beginning. Let me take you there.

The whole weird trip starts on a beautiful mid-summer morning. The blazing pants are still hours away. I'm sitting at the kitchen table checking out the movies in the newspaper. I have a date tonight. I wonder if maybe Dad does, too. He's washing a purple shirt in the sink. Except he isn't really washing it, he's watching it. Just leaning on the counter as if he isn't sure what to do next. I've noticed that a lot lately.

"It won't wash itself, Dad."

He tosses me a smile two sizes too small. He says, "According to the directions, it will." Then he holds up a pink bottle that says *Feathery Soft for Delicates*. It makes me think of Mom's stuff hanging in the bathroom. Only it's not our bathroom anymore.

"It's silk," he says. "Doesn't like to get roughed up."

Just then the timer on his wristwatch buzzes and he returns to his delicate task. I observe. Since the breakup, I've been observing him a lot. When I'm at Mom's, I observe her. I'm trying to figure out how we got to this trial separation thing. How, six weeks ago, just plain here became here and there.

"He's too polite, that papa of yours."

I watch him rinse the shirt out under cold water.

I opened up the dictionary and I said to Mom, "Polite as in having good manners or polite as in re-fined, cultivated?"

She screwed up her face. "He has always been the perfect gentleman, of course. But lately, he's ... how should I say … intimidé. He's nervous all the time as if he was having an affair or something."

"But he isn't."

She shrugged. Pouts. "He's too finicky," she said.

Gingerly, he wrings out his shirt. Is this what she means?

I looked up finicky. "So he concentrates too much on small and unimportant details?"

"Michel," she said, frowning. "Enough with the dictionary."

"I'm trying to understand."

She wrapped her arms around herself. She looked as if she was trying to understand as well, leaning on her own counter in her own kitchen.

"Suddenly it is 'everything in moderation,'" she said. "But this … this contrainte. This is not moderation. It's as if he woke up one morning and discovered he was an octopus in a boutique."

I watch him slowly wrap his fragile shirt in a fluffy yellow towel.

"'Moderation: the limiting, controlling or restricting of something so that it becomes or remains moderate.' And that's bad?"

Now she glared. "He wasn't always like this, Michel, and you know it. Just the last year or so." She poured herself a glass of wine. "Everything in moderation is fine. But you have to moderate moderation with a little joie de vivre, *non?" She sipped the wine. "He used to be a passionate man, your father."*

I closed the dictionary. I didn't want any more definitions. But I lay in bed later that night, trying to think what happened in the last year or so to change things. I became a teenager. Was it me?

Dad stands back and regards his handiwork, pleased with himself in a modest kind of way.

The phone rings. He picks it up and his eyes get big. "No!" he says. And I am rigid with fear. Something has happened to Mom. But now I see that his eyes are big with wonder not alarm. "You're kidding!" he says. Wonder transforms his face to a grin the size of July. "Really?" he says. *"Archilochus alexandri?"*

I should have guessed. It's about a bird.

"What now?" I ask. "Someone spot a dodo walking up Yonge Street?"

He shakes his head. "Nothing so large," he says, "But rare. A black-chinned hummingbird."

Right on cue, a ruby-throated hummingbird zooms to the feeder outside the kitchen window. I can see it hovering, its wings a blur, just beyond my father's shoulder. It's not such a big coincidence. They feed about every three seconds. They're the only birds in the world with ADHD.

"So this black-chin — there's only a few left?"

Dad shakes his head again. "It's not an endangered species. It's just that they summer in Texas, not Eastern Canada. This little fellow is thousands of kilometers from home."

He rubs his hands together. It's as if his whole day just took on a brighter hue. Then he glances hopefully my way.

"Want to come?"

I groan inside. When I was little, I enjoyed clambering around in other people's hedges to spy on wrens and warblers, but the thrill has gone.

Oh, but the look on his face. I check my watch. It's only ten. And after all, I want to do my part toward bringing about world peace, if only in the Whiticar family.

"Okay," I say, a little slow on the uptake. "As long as we're back by dinner."

From the look on Dad's face, that's not an option.

"Ottawa?" I say, when he explains where this tiny Texas fugitive has been sighted. "That's, like, 400 kilometers away."

"Not quite Ottawa," he quickly adds. "Some little place in the country northwest of there. Bob is going to email me a map. A place called Elphin."

I try to imagine what kind of a road map leads to somewhere called Elphin.

"Can we put it off until next weekend?"

He explains that it's a very rare occurrence and I explain how getting a date is a very rare occurrence and he explains how there'll be plenty of dates down the road and I explain that there'll be plenty of birds down the road and then he's about to play his next card but he stops midsentence, takes a deep breath and says he understands.

That's something else he does a lot lately. We hardly ever get up a good head of steam on an argument anymore before he bails. I see a flicker of tension along his jaw and realize how much this understanding costs.

Then the phone rings again. Good, I think. It's Bob to say the sighting was a hoax. But the joke's on me. It's Delia, and the date is off.

So there we are, Dad and I, speeding along old Highway 7 northbound to adventure! Bob canceled. Maybe he suddenly remembered he had a life. It's all rough and tumble up here. Bush as far as the eye can see. Rock and pine and wetland. There is a lake around every curve of the highway. Some are little more than beaver-dammed ponds littered with the gray trunks of dying trees. I find the Tragically Hip on the radio then lose them again. Even radio waves get lost in these endless woods.

This is the fringe of the Canadian Shield, the oldest mountain range in the world, worn down to low-slung hills. I wonder what that little hummingbird thought when he landed here. This isn't Texas anymore, Toto.

Dad smokes. He never used to. It's a nervous habit and being alone with me in the car seems to make him nervous. He cranks open his window and hangs half his torso outside in an attempt to save me from second-hand smoke. But that doesn't save me from the second-hand worry. I remember Mom's word. *Intimidé.* I intimidate him. And I don't know why.

He closes the window and natters about faculty politics at the university where he teaches math. Now that we only see each other every other week he saves this stuff up. I try to be interested but it's pretty dull and it never stops. Then suddenly it does.

Dad stops talking. I see his hands tighten on the wheel. There is panic in his eyes. I'm afraid he's having a stroke.

"Are you okay?"

"I'm fine," he says too quickly, training his eyes on the road. He looks as if he's going to say more and I wait. That's how I must have missed the sign. Too busy observing Dad.

YOU'VE HEARD of the back of beyond? Elphin is beyond that. It's like a trip back in time. We're climbing up into the Lanark Highlands and I keep expecting to see some Algonquin hunter standing on the shoulder staring at the cracked and pitted pavement of County Road 36, wondering how it got there. So it is all the more astounding to come upon so many cars after kilometers of nothing. Twenty-three vehicles I count, pulled well off onto the verge under a canopy of maples alive with summer breezes.

In a clearing is a tidy little log house obviously owned by the three bears. This is the object of our pilgrimage? No. Something buzzing around that neat little house. Something the size of a sugar cube, a sugar cube with attitude. There are license plates from as far away as Quebec, New York and Vermont. There's even a van from a TV station.

Dad gathers his camera equipment together and we head off to join the eager throng. Except that Dad sees a candy wrapper and has to stop to pick it up. He pockets it. He has this thing about litter.

THE BIRDERS wait patiently by the roadside until they are invited, in small clutches, to see THE BIRD. Dad bides his time, chatting with fellow birders and occasionally stooping to swoop up a gum wrapper.

The three bears turn out to be three nice hippies: Papa Hippie with a ponytail, Momma Hippie with a longer ponytail and Baby Hippie with the longest ponytail of all. They seem to enjoy the company. Mamma Hippie has baked brownies and Baby Hippie shows everyone his tree fort.

Black-chin clearly does *not* enjoy the company. He's in a foul mood. But then, in my limited experience, hummingbirds are always in a foul mood. You'd be in a foul mood if waking up in the morning was enough to kill you. It's true! Hummingbirds sometimes have heart attacks just waking up.

The little heart-attack-in-training darts around, dive-bombing the birders and dive-bombing the local ruby-throats as well. The weird thing is, it takes me a long time to distinguish this accidental tourist from the locals. I was hoping for something neon yellow with racing stripes. But Black-chin looks just like the ruby-throats as far as I can tell: long beak, bad temper. In a reverent whisper, Dad points out the purple band around the stranger's throat.

For a purple band, we have driven 317 kilometers?

Finally our turn is up and we head back out toward the road.

Goldilocks is waiting.

She's in red high heels. She has a microphone in hand, a cameraman on a chain, and from twenty meters away you can see that she's singled Dad out from the herd. He immediately lights up another cigarette.

I observe him through the smoke. He looks calm enough. No one else would know he was nervous. And suddenly, I am, too, because I can't help noticing how good-looking he is. It's not supposed to matter how your father looks. But I see Goldilocks fuss with her hair, and it makes me jumpy.

"You don't have to talk to her," I whisper.

"That would be rude," he whispers back. He takes one last long drag on his cigarette and bravely smiles for the camera.

"Ornery little cuss, isn't he?" says Goldilocks, flashing a hundred-watt smile. There are introductions all around, but Goldilocks only has eyes for Dad. "The bird attacked my cameraman," she says. "And he only weighs three grams."

Dad grins pleasantly. "He looks to me as if he weighs closer to ninety kilos."

"Oh, that is so funny," squeals Goldilocks. "Did you catch that, Ray?"

The cameraman holds up his hand to indicate he's rolling, and Goldilocks puts on her TV face.

"I'm talking to Terry Whiticar who drove all the way up here from Toronto with his son to witness this rare event. What do you think brought this little fella our way, Terry?" she asks.

Dad shrugs. "Maybe someone in Houston sneezed," he says.

Goldilocks is in raptures. She's getting good tape. I figure this must be a big step up from reading the weather.

"Some people say he might have lost his sense of direction," she says. "Others say he got caught up in a trade wind. What's your take, Terry?"

Dad looks back across the lawn to where the latest gaggle of birders is gathered in silent awe. His face becomes thoughtful.

"Maybe it wasn't an accident," he says.

Goldilocks looks surprised. "Really?"

Dad turns to her and his face is serious, almost pained. "Maybe things were just so bad back home, he had to get away."

And that's when his pants go up in flames.

Well, not flames, exactly, but they sure as heck are on fire. Remember the cigarette? Dad slipped the butt into his pocket along with all the other trash. He just didn't quite put the butt out first. Suddenly he is dancing around hitting himself and I'm running after him hitting him, too. All I can think is that I've got to put Dad out!

Sure enough, Mr. Black-chin gets in on the act, chasing us, his wings making this low whirring whistle over our heads, until Papa Hippie solves everything with a bucketful of water. It's well water from the cold clear depths of the oldest mountains in the world.

RAY GETS the whole song and dance on tape. Goldilocks takes Dad's email address so she can send him a link. Right.

"That was so stupid!" I shout, when we're back in the car. "You could have seriously hurt yourself."

Dad turns the car around and we head back down to the world.

"I'm sorry," he says.

"I don't *want* you to be sorry," I shout. "I don't *want* you to understand. I don't *want* you to be so polite that you go up in flames."

There's silence for about three-tenths of a kilometer. He reaches for his cigarettes then changes his mind. He clears his throat.

"I'm sorry for apologizing," he says.

It's a joke. I *know* it's a joke, but for some reason I bellow at him to shut up and then, before I know what's hit me, I'm crying. It's totally absurd. I sob and sniffle and basically dissolve right there on the passenger's seat.

"Where's Michel?" Mom will ask. "Oh," Dad will say. "He dissolved, sorry."

Dad is smart enough not to say anything. It's not about the fire. It's about everything. Anyway, it is through a veil of stale tears that I see the road sign. The one I missed on the way up.

"Oompah," I say, like a tuba.

Dad says nothing.

I turn as we pass the sign and read it out loud. "'Turn Right for Oompah.' Why does that ring a bell?"

Still nothing. But I notice Dad's hands tighten on the wheel. He's wearing pants he borrowed from Papa Hippie. Faded yellow jeans with crazy patches on them. His face looks kind of yellow, too. We're driving into the sunset.

"It's Ompah," he says at last. "To rhyme with stomp."

I sniff and wipe my wet face. "You mean to rhyme with stompa," I correct him.

His smile is grim. He shakes his head as if he's trying to jiggle something loose in his skull. Then all of a sudden he slows down the car.

"Dad?"

No answer. We just roll to a stop. My window's down and the evening air is filled with cricket song and the screech of blue jays.

"The Ompah Stomp," he says. "The big end-of-summer hoedown."

Then I remember. "Ompah. Of course! That's where you grew up."

He shakes his head. "The road to Ompah," he says, as if there is an important difference. He seems lost in thought. I sit back, feeling empty and exhausted.

I notice that we've pulled to a stop right at the intersection of Highway 509, the road to Ompah. There's a big homemade sign at the intersection: "Blue Skies," it reads, with an arrow pointing north.

"So that's where those blue skies got to," I say.

I look at Dad. He's ticking. It's his brain, I think, ticking like a time bomb. Then I notice it's just his fingernail on the steering wheel. His eyes look as if he's watching a horror movie and it's come to the scene with the knife and the bathtub. I want to reach out and touch him, but I resist the urge. I don't want him to go off.

He must be remembering his parents. They died years and years ago, as far as I know. There's no pictures, no cards. I don't think he was a happy kid. Watching him now, he doesn't *look* like a happy kid.

He clears his throat. *"Archilochus alexandri,"* he says so quietly I can hardly hear him. The Laurentian Shield gets a little older, erodes just a little more before he speaks again. "Maybe that bird was sent to me," he says.

Now I'm really worried. Can a fire in your pants actually fry your brain? But he chuckles — seems to guess what I'm thinking.

"Sorry," he says. "I'm not making much sense."

I shrug. "Yeah, well, join the club."

It turns out he's still thinking about the Black-chin. "Nothing else would have brought me up this way," he says. "I don't know why I've avoided it so long." He looks at me squarely. "Do you mind if we pay a little visit?" he asks.

I groan, partly from hunger and partly from apprehension, but I keep it to myself.

THERE'S ANOTHER homemade sign a little farther up the road. "You're almost there!" it says. Blue Skies, I guess. Is that where we're going? Looking at Dad's bleak expression, I don't think so.

Then suddenly he puts on his indicator light, slows down and pulls off 509 onto a dirt driveway. I catch sight of the name on the battered black mailbox. The letters are cracked and peeling but the ghost of them remains. "Whiticar," it says.

The driveway climbs through stunted trees and moss-covered granite glowing pink in the setting sun. The bush closes in around us. Tall weeds brush the sides of the car. Then we come to a clearing littered with cannibalized cars and scrawny chickens that flutter out of our path as we come to a stop in a cloud of our own dust. Before us sits a rambling tarpaper shack. There's a porch with a bowed and rusted tin roof held up by arthritic log posts.

A man is standing in the shadows on the stoop. He steps out into the sunlight. His shadow is a lot longer than he is. He's wearing filthy gray work pants held up with a length of twine, and a T-shirt stained yellow around the armholes. He comes down the steps. He's got a farmer's tan; his lower arms are oven-roasted, his upper arms are as white as bone. He's got a grizzled gray beard, a balding head and there's a scowl brewing on his face.

I glance nervously at Dad for some clue. An uncle? A second cousin three hundred times removed? Dad is staring straight ahead at the unfriendly looking geezer, as if he's in a trance.

This other Whiticar is making his way toward us, kicking at chickens that cross his path. Dad opens the door and steps out and quickly I do the same. We slam our doors shut simultaneously, as if we're Starsky and Hutch arriving on the scene of the crime but in a white and timid-looking Honda.

Mr. Chicken-Kicker may be short but he's as solid as a forty-gallon drum. His arms and rounded shoulders look strong, despite his age. He's got a long rod in his hand. Some part of a tractor, I guess: oily and rusty, with a chain at the end. He stops, looks Dad up and down, his scornful eyes resting on the faded yellow jeans.

"Does this look like a music festival?" he says. He sounds like he just ate a bucketful of gravel. "It's another mile to Blue Skies, asshole," he adds. Dad doesn't answer. "Are ya stoned?" the old man shouts. He has reached the front of our car now and he raises his rod as if he's going to strike the grill.

"How about I put your lights out," he shouts. "Will that wake ya up?"

He brings his improvised weapon down hard on the ground. I gasp and a smirk lights up his face. And then it dawns on me who this swamp creature must be. My father is slim and tall but the flecks of gray in his black hair are the same as the gray of this man's beard. My father will one day grow bald in the same way as this man. And, looking at my father now, I see an exact reflection of the other's anger. This is my grandfather and he's anything but dead. He also seems to have realized who it is he's talking to.

"Well, well, well," he says. "What brings *you* here?"

"A bird."

Grandfather cackles.

"A woman?"

"No," says my father. "A real bird. A nasty little bird a long way from home."

Old Mr. Whiticar squints suspiciously. "What in hell's name are ya talking about?" he demands.

"I'm explaining how I ended up here, " says my father, and his voice is so brittle, I worry for him. "These pants — they're part of the story," he says, soldiering on. "A friend — a kind stranger — lent them to me when my own pants went up in smoke. And do you know why that happened? No, of course you don't. Well, it was because I was trying to make things nice. Pretty stupid, eh? Trying to make everything nice."

The old man shook his head in disgust. "You're a frigging lunatic," he says. And with the salutations out of the way, he turns his attention to me. "This yours?" he asks Dad, as if I were a used car.

"This is Michel, my son," says Dad.

The old man assesses me the way a butcher might weigh up a side of lamb. "He looks soft," he says. He makes the word sound like the first symptom of a terminal disease. "Is that why you gave him a girl's name?"

"He's a good boy," says my father. "A wonderful boy. But I wouldn't expect you of all people to recognize that."

Old Mr. Whiticar doesn't favor his son with so much as a glance. His eyes are trained on me and filled with mischief. "Hear the way he talks to his old man?" he says. "Nice, eh?"

I don't answer. I feel as if I've fallen down a rabbit hole. The Mad Hatter is moving now, coming around to my side of the car.

"Does he bad-mouth me a lot, kid?"

Even if I could speak, the words would never make it to the top of this pit I'm in. He leans against the car, shaking his head contemptuously.

"You're a meek little son of a bitch," he says. "Does he beat ya?"

I look at Dad. I want him to do something — to at least *say* something — but his mouth is clamped shut. I see that flicker of a pulse along his jaw, like a worm under the skin. I turn to his father and shake my head.

"He hit *me* once," says the old man rubbing his belly. "Can you believe it?" He sneers. "He only tried it once."

He slides his oil-stained hand along the car as he comes toward me. I back up — can't help it

— until my hand is resting on the door handle. He smiles a bully's smile of satisfaction. And that grimace is like a toehold for me, somehow, at the very bottom of my pit. I start to climb.

The man sidles up closer, glancing sideways to appraise how this is going over with Dad. Dad watches, nothing more, and I can see the horror movie still playing in his eyes.

Now, Grandfather Whiticar is close enough that I can smell the sourness of him. At close quarters I see the bitterness in his pale blue eyes.

"I'd watch him, if I were you," he says to me in a stage whisper. He indicates my father with a wag of his head. "Got a temper on him like a wild turkey."

I clear my throat. "I can see where he gets it from."

Grandfather's amused face darkens. "What's that, boy?"

I let go of the door handle and step tentatively toward him. "If my father has a temper, I can see why."

The old man rubs his bearded chin. He looks hard at me, re-evaluating the merchandise. "Your dad there, he got real insolent round about your age." His face is right up close to mine, except he's shorter, and he has to look up ever so slightly. "Don't pay to be rude to me, boy," he says poking himself in the chest. "Not a bright idea."

I nod. "I think I understand."

"Good," he says, hoisting up his pants, as if I've passed a test. And now he looks across the car toward my father. "Big shot over there never figured it out. Thought he was something special. Thought the sun shone out of his scrawny butt."

I interrupt him. "No, I meant I think I understand why my father never bad-mouths you. Never talks about you at all."

"He doesn't?"

"Never. Not a word."

The old man looks wary, "All right, bright spark. Tell me why?"

I make myself look right into his stony eyes. "Because you aren't worth talking about."

I see his hand jerk — the one holding the weapon — but I'm quicker than he is. My foot comes down hard on the chain, and the whole rusty thing leaps from his hand and clatters to the ground.

He grabs his wrist in pain. "You little bastard," he says and steps toward me with his meaty hand raised.

"Michel!" Dad shouts and the cry is enough to stop the old man in his tracks. He sounds so angry, we both turn to look at him. But Dad is staring only at me.

"Apologize to your grandfather," he demands.

I can't believe it. His eyes are filled with an unholy rage.

"You heard him," says Whiticar, poking me in the shoulder. "It's the first sensible thing he's said since he got here."

Hearing his gravelly voice wakes me up. A whole tumble of things make sense all at once. I look at my father and there is so much more than rage in his eyes. There is a furious spark of defiance and a wicked glint of humor. I get it. I get it all in one atom-splitting instant. And I know *exactly* what I have to do. I turn to face my aggressor. He looks smug.

"I'm so sorry, Granddad," I say humbly and submissively. "I didn't mean to be impolite."

It works like a charm. It *is* a charm, because when I glance at my father he looks as if he's been released from a spell. The horror movie is over. It's as if my apology has slammed a door in the old man's face. He can't get at my father anymore. He can't get at either of us.

We climb back into the Honda. When we turn the car around to go, Whiticar is still standing in the same place, still rubbing the wrist of his right arm. But in my last glimpse of him in the side-view mirror, he looks frail, as if anger was all that was holding him together. All his beautiful wickedness.

As THE summer night settles around the car, Dad tells me of the time he punched his father. The old man had been terrorizing Mrs. Whiticar and Dad couldn't take it any longer. He hit him and knocked him down. Then he left and never came home again. He was thirteen, like me. He wrote to his mother, worried about her. She wrote back and told him that she could look after herself but she could not look after him, so it was just as well he was gone.

Silence descends upon us, but it's a companionable silence. Dad never once reaches for his smokes. It's a long time before he talks again.

"When we started fighting, it frightened me," he says.

"I bet it did. He's so mean, so strong."

"I mean when *you and I* started fighting," says my father.

I turn to look at him. "Fighting? Us?"

"Arguing," he says. "You know. Questioning me. Daring to have your own opinion. You had always been this helpful little guy who liked to hang out with his father, run errands, help with chores. Then, out of nowhere, there's this cocky stranger rolling his eyes. It caught me off guard. I was outraged. And my anger frightened me to death." He pauses and a spasm of resentment contorts his face. But by now I know it's not me he's angry with. "I was afraid I was becoming him," he says.

I stare out through my own reflection at the night. I look back at Dad. I see him differently. We have traveled so far today.

"You *are* allowed to disagree with me, Dad," I say to him. "As long as you realize that I'm *always* right, I'm sure we'll get along just fine."

His face breaks into a moonlit smile. "I understand," he says.

HE WAKES me as we fly down the Don Valley Parkway. He's found an oldies station playing "Wouldn't It Be Nice" by the Beach Boys.

"I was thinking we should get a pizza," he says. He makes it sound as if he's decided we should buy a Ferrari. "Maybe we could drop by your mom's place. Tell her where we've been. You think she'd be up for a party?"

I rub the sleep out of my eyes and check the clock on the dashboard. It's coming on to 2:00 a.m. What was it he said? *Tell her where we've been.* And through the muzziness of sleep a bright and glittering penny drops.

"Mom doesn't know about him, does she."

Dad slowly shakes his head. "I didn't want to burden her."

"But you're going to tell her now, right? She has to know."

He nods. "You're right. Will you help me?"

I think hard. Then I take a deep breath. "What kind of a pizza, Dad?"

He gives it some serious thought. "A really big pizza seems in order. With banana peppers and anchovies and both kinds of olives and double cheese?"

I nod again. "We'd better get some ice cream, as well," I suggest.

"Good thinking," he says.

I yawn and settle comfortably in my seat. I look ahead down the empty freeway. It won't be dawn for hours yet, but if I strain my eyes, I swear I can almost see the light.

IN A HOUSE BUILT OUT OF DRAGONFLY WINGS

THERE IS an overgrown trail off the Foxtail Road that leads down through maple and silver birch to a brook. It is an old logging trail, but Jess calls it the Haunted Road and she calls the brook the Stream of Dreams. She says there is a tiny house on a rock below the Teacup Falls. The house is really a jail, she says, and it's made out of dragon-fly wings, and there is a girl who was kidnapped by the gremlins trapped inside it.

"Does your guitar really have strings made of cats' guts?" she asks Walker.

Walker shakes his head. "Nylon," he says. She glares, chooses not to believe him.

"Well, I think the door of the dragonfly house is made out of cat-gut strings, anyway, but they are enchanted so that the girl inside can't get through them. When she rattles her cage it sounds kind of pretty, though. For a prison."

On and on, Jess rattles. And Walker listens and Walker hears about as much as any eighteen-year-old ever does a ten-year-old.

He knows the brook, the Teacup Falls, though it had always been just "the falls" to him. Lying on the bank there on a spring day not unlike this one when he was about Jess's age, he watched an otter cruise downstream toward him. He recalls it vividly now. He remembers knowing even then with all the certainty of childhood that the otter was playing. Not hunting, not building a den or on the make — not working. Playing.

He used that otter once in an argument with his father.

"Animals don't play," his father told him with all the certainty of adulthood. Then he issued Walker a dire warning. "Let me tell you this, my friend: no wild animal dies of old age."

Walker wasn't sure what he meant. But his father had rhymed it off as if it were the coup de grâce in their quarrel. It was only later that Walker learned it wasn't his father's idea, anyway; it was a quote from Ernest Thompson Seton, whose nature stories were almost as dreary as his father.

He remembers that quarrel now and thinks of how little play there was in his father. Maybe that was the reason his mother divorced him. Then Walker thinks of play and wonders how much of it there is in his own life at college. His guitar, of course; weekend parties; beer; girls. But even that seems like work sometimes. Has he died, then, the child in him?

Gleefully, he recalls the otter, how it came *that* close to where he lay in wait, hardly breathing, before it noticed him and fled overland in terror. But he doesn't recall any dragonfly real estate. He was never that kind of a kid.

Walker is tagging along not for the fairy house but because it is spring. Spring is his agenda, and that long-ago otter, bright again in his mind's eye, poking its whiskery nose up through the residue of text books and exam papers littering the floor of his exhausted brain.

Wild leeks are on his agenda, too. There were leeks up this way; sharp, green shoots in the wadded carpet of the forest floor.

And finally, there is Jess. It has been a rough term and Jess is powerful medicine.

THE MOON shines foolishly in the middle of the afternoon sky.

"Do you think there could be something like derring-don't?" asks Jess. "Kind of the opposite of derring-do."

Walker is amused. "Derring-don't? Why not. Someone filled with the desire *not* to do anything adventurous?"

"Yeah," says Jess. "That's exactly what I was thinking."

"Then how about free won't?" says Walker, caught up in Jess's enthusiasm for everything under the frail thumbprint of a moon. "I guess that would be the freedom to *not* be able to do what you want to do."

Side by side, Jess and Walker slog through the sodden leaves, eviscerated of color by the winter. "Are you thinking about your princess in her dragonfly jail?" he asks.

"She's not a princess, Walk, just a girl. And I

wasn't thinking about her just now. I was trying to think what free won't is. Is it the opposite of free will? Is that the joke? Because I don't know what free will is."

Walker chuckles to himself. To explain free will to Jess would be like explaining how to get home to Lassie. "How do we get in these conversations, Jess?"

Jess shrugs. "I guess it's because I was talking about derring-do and derring-don't, but I can't remember why anymore."

"Oh," says Walker. And then he stops and says, "Shhh." For the sound of the brook has come to him.

They are quiet: Jess with the hope of catching gremlins at work, Walker with the hope of catching otters at play.

There are rocks, a careless stairway down into the Teacup. Silently Walker and Jess make their way to where the brook, having splashed through an obstacle course of boulders and dead trees, cascades down a series of rapids and pools to the swampy, wooded valley below.

And because they are so diligent in their silence, they hear a sound above the noise of splashing water that is neither fairy folk nor anything quite natural. A metal creaking, a clanking sound. A man's laugh. Jess skibbles back up to the rim of the Teacup, and Walker follows awkwardly on all fours.

Down below and only a stone's throw away through the still-naked trees stands a half-ton truck, its back to them, its body sprung high for off-road sport. There are two men standing on the tailgate, tipping a forty-gallon drum. A thick stream of black sludge gushes out onto the ground. There are four drums in all.

"What the hell!" says Walker.

"We have to get their license number," whispers Jess.

Walker nods in agreement and starts to calculate in his mind whether the men have just started or whether they're just finishing; whether he and Jess can make it back through the woods in time to intercept the vehicle out on the open road; whether they can make it look unintentional; whether he has a pencil.

Jess, however, is untroubled by strategy. She's up over the lip of the Teacup and skibbling down the hill toward the men, darting, stumbling — half-falling — from tree to tree. Walker prepares for trouble.

But it doesn't come. The men finish their business, wipe their hands on their grimy overalls, oblivious to the witness of their crime. The engine roars and the truck lurches up what must be another logging trail, for these woods were logged heavily in the old days. The truck's wheels spin in the mud with no load any longer over the back tires. By the time Walker joins Jess, she's writing the license plate number with a rock on the slimy backside of a piece of birch bark.

"Nice work," says Walker. He wants to scold her for her rashness, but he stops himself. He doesn't want to be accused of derring-don't.

She hands him the birch-bark evidence and looks anywhere but at the oil spill.

"Neat, eh!" she says. And Walker notices for the first time they are standing in an old junkyard, an abandoned dump site on the edge of swampy ground. He can't remember ever knowing it was there before. Jess seems delighted. There are bedsprings and bowed pieces of ancient farm equipment. There is an icebox with its doors torn off, and a cracked woodstove with weeds growing in the firebox like newly minted flames.

It is an old dump, its rusty feet still trapped in hard gray snow. It is overgrown. There are no

Coke cans, no plastics. Nothing new but a small lake of black effluent.

Jess explores. She liberates a steering wheel and drives it around the dump. She tries on a tractor seat as if it were the latest in spring helmets. Walker stands on the shore of the inky sludge, feeling somehow abandoned.

"Look at this!" cries Jess. She has found the carcass of a telephone booth. "This must be pre-Columbian," she says, for Columbus has figured prominently in her schoolwork this term.

She kneels down and picks through broken glass and drags out a matted coat of animal pelts. "No, it's older," she says. "Probably Stone Age. Look at this, Walk, look. There's a label inside the collar. 'Property of Og the Caveman.'"

Walker cannot speak. It is shady down here, colder. All the spring seems to have been wrung out of the day.

"Maybe he was phoning home," Jess rattles on, "to tell Ogetta that the woolly mammoth hunt wasn't going so well when — boom! — he was hit by a meteorite."

"Boom!" says Walker. "Bloody boom ..."

Jess makes a face at him, at his apparent bad mood. She slips her arm into one of the coat's tattered sleeves. She is tentative, fearing perhaps that her fingers might make contact with some of Og, or a mouse, or a slug family. Triumphantly, her fist pokes through the opening. Then her left arm fearlessly navigates the damp reaches of the other sleeve.

"This used to be a whole herd of raccoons," she says. "Imagine."

"Do you have any idea what vermin probably live in that thing now?" says Walker.

Jess looks down at the tattered hem hanging around her ankles. She sniffs. "It stinks," she says, but makes no move to take it off. Then she has to skip-step aside, for a rivulet of the oily puddle has found its way to her.

"What is it?" she asks, wrinkling her nose.

"Gunk," says Walker. "Lubricant soup. Crank-case oil, goop of all kinds — you name it."

Jess joins Walker beside the still, dark pond. She growls, "The devil damn thee black, thou cream-faced loon."

THE SUN is low on Foxtail Road. Jess spins around to make her new-old coat twirl. It is so heavy she almost falls over. "I think it belongs to Superman," she says.

"What happened to Og?"

Jess snorts. "Oh, come on, Walk. As if they had phones in the Stone Age."

But Walker doesn't rise to the bait. He is filled with chagrin. And Jess's gaiety suddenly annoys him.

"You know how he changes in phone booths?" she says. "Well, he must have left it there, see. Then robbers came and stole the booth before he got back."

"Sure," says Walker. "Right."

JESS IS Walker's half-sister, his mother's other kid. His father never remarried. Too busy. Their mother is away right now. She is an actress. She is playing Lady Macbeth in Winnipeg. That's where the "cream-faced loon" came from. *Macbeth.* Jess has learned all the lines. There was even a chance she'd get to play Macduff's son, but the director's nephew got the part. She would have loved it. "Thou li'st thou shag ear'd villain!" She is not a child of ordinary curses.

Jess's father, Steve, phones the police when they tell him what they've seen. The police tell Steve it's not in their jurisdiction; he should phone the provincial police. The provincial police tell him to phone the offices of the municipality. But the office is closed.

"I'll phone first thing in the morning," says Steve.

Jess sits on the kitchen floor in Superman's discarded furs, absorbed in getting her Barbie doll into a fur coat of her own. She pushes too hard, tears one of Barbie's sleeves.

"Hell-kite," she says.

"Jess!" says Steve. "And will you *please* get that wretched coat out of the house."

WALKER DREAMS of an otter. There is no one lying in wait, no one to scare it off. It is his dream, but he is not in it. Suddenly the otter pricks up its ears, listens, scampers out of the stream, terrified. By what, what? Then Walker is sitting up in bed, falling out of bed, his feet tied up in the bed clothes. Someone is screaming.

It's not a dream. It's Jess. Her father is the first to reach her.

"O, O, O," she sobs, wringing her hands. She trembles in his arms. "Everything will be black," she says. "The girl, the girl. She's trapped."

"I'll get you a glass of water," says Walker. When he arrives back, Jess is a bit calmer but disoriented.

She takes the glass from him but stares at it suspiciously. Won't drink it. Won't.

"What are we going to do, Walk?" she says, her voice small and pleading. "The goop will all be gone by the time anyone bothers to go see it."

Walker sighs. "I'll go get a jar of it, okay? As evidence."

"Okay."

"First thing tomorrow."

"No. Now."

"It's midnight, Jess. Tomorrow. First thing."

"No, no, no!" says Jess. Suddenly she's out of bed and heading for the door, fighting off all attempts to restrain her. Walker and her father block the way. She is out of control. No pleading, no sweet language will contain her. Around and around her room she tromps, over the bed, down the other side. She is acting out of her dream, urgent, unmanageable.

She has sneaked the raggedy coat up to her room. Now she slips it on. She points her finger at her two pursuers, stopping them in their tracks.

"This is Superman's coat!" she warns them. She is shaking with rage. Then — maybe it's the looks on their faces, or maybe she has only just woken up — suddenly it's too funny and she is laughing. Then crying. Then they are holding her.

Then somehow, though he cannot quite believe he agreed to it, Walker is out in the blustery spring night, in boots and a winter parka, with a flashlight and an empty Miracle Whip bottle, on a goop-gathering mission.

The moon — confused by spring — set before nightfall. There is only starlight to accompany Walker on his lonely mission. Stars and the wind in the pines and the peepers in the lowland. And a barred owl barking like a moon-throated dog.

His mind is full of Jess wringing her hands like Lady Macbeth; sleep-walking, unable to wash away the blood stains from her own murderous hands. This is not a comforting thought.

And it's a great deal worse when Walker veers off the Foxtail Road into the woods, the closer darkness of the Haunted Road. He curses Jess and her fertile imagination — her naming of things — for it has infected him.

Things move in the woods, creak and snap, stirred by the wind. Things skitter for shelter, stalked by night hunters. Branches break underfoot or reach out and brush his cheek with alarming familiarity. Even the sound of Teacup Falls when it comes to him at last holds little pleasure. It is too loud, covers up too much else. Walker finds himself flinging the flimsy beam of his flashlight every which way, manufacturing monsters in the tangle of shadows and wind-fingered undergrowth. A bear. Wolves. Three witches. Two men in overalls with oil-dirty hands.

Here are his and Jess's tracks from the afternoon, sinking into the boggy ground along the stream's bank. Down the rocky steps, below the wind into the sheltered dip of land Jess calls the Teacup.

From here he will make his way down to the valley floor and the dump. He just needs a little rest before making his descent. He sits on a boulder by the brook, trying to collect his racing thoughts. He shivers, for this moonless April night is still fat with winter.

A clattering sound comes to him from farther down the stream. He stops a raccoon in his flashlight's beam.

It is perched on a table rock that juts out over the falling water. One paw is deep inside something that looks to Walker at first glance like a hive of some kind but that glitters faintly in the light. The raccoon is transfixed by the beam. Then hastily it withdraws its paw, something white in its grasp.

"Shoo!" whispers Walker. And the raccoon jumps down from the rock, dropping whatever it has won from the hive-like thing, and races off into the forest.

Walker tracks the raccoon with his flashlight until it is out of sight, then he swings his beam back to the construction on the rock. It is not a hive but an inverted bowl-shaped thing.

Walker slides down the bank on the seat of his pants. The scent of wild leeks rises up around him. Finally he stops beside a small mystery, a dome-shaped creation. The structure sways in a gust of wind. Impulsively, Walker reaches out to catch it, fearing it will be whisked clear off its foundation, whirled away into the night. But it is fixed to the rock. There is a tear in its side where the raccoon has been at work. Caught in the rocks at the foot of the stone table, Walker finds a small white naked doll.

He peers closer at the construct. It is made, it seems, entirely from dragonfly wings. Bending low, so that his chin hovers just above the cold granite table, Walker shines his light through the transparent walls. There is a bed made of twigs tied together with woven grass. The bed is weighted down with a beautiful rounded stone pillow.

There is a handkerchief bedspread half dragged off the little bed onto the floor of the dragonfly house. With each gust of wind, the house seems to breath. In and out. So fragile and yet so strong.

Walker's fears desert him. He is filled with astonishment, with wonder. He hunkers down close to the rock out of the wind. He remembers how every year the dragonflies come. Their coming is a celebration for it marks the end of blackfly season. The dragonflies are the cavalry of early summer. Whirlybird knights. They come in scores, gobbling blackflies by day and resting on the west wall of the house in the evening, as if recharging their batteries in the setting sun.

When they are killed, as many of them are, by passing cars, Jess picks up their broken bodies from along the Foxtail Road; she plucks them off the car grills and out of the mesh of screen doors and windows. She collects them in a blue and emerald-green pottery bowl. He has seen it on her windowsill. And now she has built this house, though how she has accomplished it, Walker cannot tell.

Another gust of wind smacks the gossamer walls. It wobbles but does not fly apart as Walker fears it must. It just breathes quietly, in and out like a sleeping mouth. Walker looks closely at the tiny doll baby in his palm, pockets it. Then he sees that the raccoon has left something behind: oily paw prints on the table rock. With new resolve, he makes his way down to the dump. He manages to fill most of the bottle with goop-soaked earth.

THE MUNICIPAL offices tell them to phone the Ministry of the Environment. The Ministry of the Environment says they'll look into it. And they do. The investigator even drops around to report. The license plate number belongs to a vehicle owned by an automobile establishment. The investigator cannot divulge the owner's name, but he has visited the establishment.

"They're properly registered," he says. "They've got what's called a waste generator number," he says. "That means they are required by law to have all hazardous waste removed by a licensed company. They have a receipt of a pick-up on Tuesday. They're too small an operation to have produced even a single drum of waste since then, let alone four," he says.

Jess scowls at the investigator. "Well, they did!"

"That may be so," says the investigator. "But it seems the owner is plagued by youths trespassing on his property, playing in his wrecking yard.

Stealing things. He's had to run them off quite a few times and he seems to think there are a few of those kids who wouldn't mind making things hot for him, if they had the chance."

It takes Walker a moment to digest this news, pick up on the inference. "We're not making this up," he says. "You saw the spill yourself."

The investigator shrugs. "I did. And I believe what you're telling me. But the fine for this kind of illegal dumping is pretty steep. If we try to prosecute, this guy is going to claim it's all a frame-up. We've only got circumstantial evidence. It's his word against yours.

"If you could get photographs, then we'd have something to work with," says the investigator. He asks them to keep their eyes open. Then he's gone.

"Hell-kite!" says Jess.

"Now, now," says Steve. "He's done what he can."

"I didn't mean him," says Jess, "I mean Carmody's Auto Wrecking."

Walker and Steve stare at her, mouths agape.

"Well, that's who he's talking about," says Jess.

And so the story unfolds a bit more. Jess recognized the men making the dump when she saw them up close. She recognized the truck, too.

They work for Carmody's Auto Wrecking up on the French Line.

"We go there sometimes after school," she says. "They never caught me, though. And we *don't* steal stuff!" she says. "We just play Freedom Fighters in the dead cars. It's just a game."

Then, before anyone can say anything adultish, she heads for her room. "It's not as if we were killing anyone," she says.

Walker isn't sure what to do and so he does nothing. There are summer job interviews to go to and old school friends to visit. There are errands to run and a leftover paper to write for school. And there is Jess to visit with and babysit when Steve's away. They play cards at night, Spite & Malice. She is merciless.

What Walker doesn't know, because Jess doesn't tell him, is that she has declared a personal war on Carmody's Auto Wrecking. She is a warrior for the Stream of Dreams.

She bikes up to Carmody's every day after school. She stands in full view of the office window in her invincible Superman coat until Carmody yells at her to vamoose. Then she crosses the road and marches back and forth in front of his property or plays provocatively with the flap on his mailbox until he yells some more.

She makes a sandwich board. *Looking for a large oil spill?* it says on the front. Then on the back it says, *Just call Carmody for free home delivery.*

"I'm calling the cops," Carmody bawls at her.

"Good," she says.

But he doesn't.

Then she enlists some willing friends. They play the wrecking yard as if it were a great noisy instrument of torture. They pull out all the stops. They bang on wrecked car doors and yodel through improvised megaphones. Kids' stuff.

Carmody and his men chase them away.

She steals out of bed one night and spray-paints his office window. *Environment Killer.*

She prints up a flyer spelling out Carmody's crime in detail. She and her friends deliver it all over the neighborhood. That's when Carmody really does call the cops. Jess is there waiting for them. The cop bends Jess's ear. He drives her home. Walker is the only one there right then. The cop tells Walker what she's been up to. He tells Walker to have Jess's father contact him. He issues her a dire warning.

"Shag ear'd villain," she says when the cop car leaves.

And Walker is terribly proud of Jess and terribly sad. Because, to his mind, it is not a game anymore. Among his sins, Carmody has stolen Jess's childhood. That's what Walker thinks and he burns with frustration. But he is wrong about Jess. She is playing hard, devoted to her game. He worries. He thinks of Jess's miraculous house by the Teacup Falls, and he wishes his mother were home. Jess is so like her. And he is not. He is not.

Jess goes underground. She spies, lurks, prowls, slinks, skulks and glides between the rusting hulks of Carmody's wrecked kingdom. She sees a truck come to take away Carmody's hazardous waste, pumping it up from a holding tank. But there is goop and gunk the licensed company will not take. She sees the man from the licensed company do some kind of a test and shake his head. Won't take it. Then, when he has gone, Jess watches it being carted off to a shack at the farthest, most overgrown corner of Carmody's vast lot.

"Damned PCPs," she hears one of Carmody's oafs swearing.

141

Then one day, just around closing, she watches Carmody's men load up the half-ton with four more drums of waste. She bikes home filled with fire.

IT IS THE first time Walker has returned to the Teacup Falls since the night of no moon when he scared away the raccoon and discovered a house built out of dragonfly wings.

But this time Jess and he are armed with sleeping bags, hot milky coffee in a flask and egg sandwiches. They are armed with cameras and Walker's phone. It is drizzling rain.

The truck comes at midnight. Walker phones the police and when he feels enough time has passed, when the cops must be on their way, he lets Jess loose. She slips from the safety of the Teacup and flits from tree to tree like some avenging fairy, flashing photographs as the sludge slops from the drum and Carmody's men yell curses into the night and try to hurry up, and spill goop on their pants and boots, and try to figure out how many assailants they are up against, for they feel utterly surrounded. Jess circles them everywhere, drawing a noose of popping camera flashes around their villainy. They are trapped by her.

The police arrive. The arrest is made.

"It'll be the car-squisher for those guys," says Jess with evident satisfaction as she and Walker gather up their gear. Walker almost suggests they spend the night in this enchanted place. But they are soaked. And through his elation pokes the bones of a dreadful weariness.

He scans the ground with his flashlight to see if they've forgotten anything. His beam finds its way down to the dragonfly house. He stares at it, tattered a bit around the edges, dented by the rain, but still intact.

"What?" says Jess.

Then Walker stares at her with such obvious admiration that even in the dark she can feel it. She blushes, and even in the dark he sees it.

"What holds it together?" he says.

Jess smiles. "Just something I found in Mum's old actor's make-up kit," she says. "Spirit gum."

JACK

THERE WAS a dead ermine in the bottom of the garbage pail. I didn't know that's what it was until Old Man Sunday told me. I picked up its frozen body with my gloved hands. It was so stiff you could hold it by its tail, straight out like a white sword. I put it in a handy berry basket and marched down the drive.

There'd been a new snowfall. You could see the ermine's tracks on the driveway right up to the corner of the old outhouse, where we keep the trash. My own tracks led me down the hill and up the next and round the bend to where Sunday lived in a house he had built from scratch out of anything he could find. He was in his workshop when I got there.

"This here's an ermine," he said. "A stoat in its winter coat."

There were stoats in *The Wind in the Willows.* Took over Toad's place. This one was all in white except for the end of his tail, which was black, as if winter hadn't quite made it all the way to the end of him.

"Your cardinals wear 'em," he said.

I looked at the little critter. It was about nine inches long from its nose to the black tip of its tail, but there wasn't much to it, weight-wise. It was slim, lithe — or at least it looked like it would have been when it was alive. I couldn't quite imagine how a cardinal would wear one. Draped across its shoulders? I sure couldn't imagine a bird flying very far with an ermine on board.

Sunday must have seen the look on my face as I tried to work it out. "Not those kind of cardinals. The ones in Rome that flock around the Pope. You ever seen them?"

This was getting a long way from the creature in the berry basket, its eyes glazed white, its tiny paws curled up. I shook my head and Old Man Sunday chuckled.

"Well, anyway," he said. "Them cardinals in Rome, they wear red, see. Red robes. But in winter you'll see some of 'em wearing a cope of white fur around their neck, on their shoulders. To keep 'em warm, I guess."

"It didn't work for this guy," I said.

Sunday shook his head. Picked up the ermine with his bare hand. Strong, knotty hands. "Nope." He put the ermine down and scratched his bearded chin. "Probably chased a mouse into your garbage can," he said.

"Some squirrel chewed a hole in the lid. It wasn't a very big hole."

He nodded, as if he'd seen it all before. "Big enough for a critter to get in, hungry. Too small to get out, full."

Old Man Sunday said stuff like that all the time. Stuff you could almost imagine on a bumper sticker.

"You want it?" I asked.

"Sure," he said. "He's a nice specimen. Thanks."

I hadn't noticed the ermine was a "he." Seemed easier when it was just an it. I took off my gloves to hang them from the woodstove to dry.

"That looks nasty," said Sunday. He was looking at the scratches across the back of my right hand.

"It doesn't hurt much," I said.

"Looks like a wall ran into you," he said. Then he looked into my eyes and waited. I looked down at the dead ermine, didn't say anything.

He took the berry basket from me and transferred the animal to a plastic freezer bag, then opened up his big old deep freeze. It was one of those king-sized ones and it was chock-full of dead animals and birds. A brown thrasher that had broken its neck flying into a window, a raven that had smacked into a car. A roadkill rabbit, a fox that died of rabies, a skunk who maybe died of his own smell — all kinds of critters. Anyone in the valley who found a dead creature that wasn't rotting or mangled took it to Sunday. He kept them to use as models for his wood carvings. People said Old Man Sunday brought those animals back to life with his knives and palm chisels, his spoon gouges and V-tools.

When my grandad died a couple years back, I had this dream where I was carrying him to Sunday, which was pretty funny on account of me being scrawny and only ten back then. That kind of thing happens in dreams. You can carry really heavy things. Anyway, in this dream, I walked all the way over to Sunday's. I wanted him to bring Grandad back to life.

Jack

When I told Mom about it, she smiled and said, "That's called magical thinking."

IT SNOWED again that night. Lying in my bed I listened to the quiet. We lived out of town so there was never much noise at night, but there's nothing quieter than snow. I found myself thinking of that stoat-turned-ermine, the black tip of its tail — no, *his* tail.

"You call the male a Jack," Sunday had said. "The female's a Jill."

If Jack had lived, maybe this snowfall would have been the one to finally turn him white all the way to the tip of his tail.

I thought of him, sleek and fast, chasing some mouse or shrew into the garbage can through that hole eaten into the plastic top. Then I thought of him not being able to get out. Trapped in there. Freezing to death. I shuddered and pulled my blankets up around me. Outside, the wind picked up and hurled snow at my window. So much for a quiet night. Then again, a snow day would be good.

I DIDN'T hate seventh grade. I used to like school okay, until Dougal Ashur came along. The thing is, he had always been there, just another nobody special — a town guy who'd won the growth gene pool. He was testing out how big he was on me. Doug the Thug I called him, but not to his face. I couldn't remember when he'd started hitting me. Steering me into walls, hurling a tennis ball at my back, tripping me, shouldering me extra hard. "Oops, sorry, Mr. Clean. Hope I didn't put a crease in your shirt."

"You are a bit of a neat freak," said Candace, the girl I always sat with on the bus.

"Is that what this is all about?"

She looked sideways at me and smiled. "Maybe you should stop combing your hair." She reached up to scruffle it and I pushed her hand away. She giggled. "See what I mean?" she said.

My dad's a writer. He talks a lot about a character in a story having to have genuine motivation. "You can't just make your character do something because the story needs him to," he'd say. "There's got to be a believable reason your character would act this way or that way." So when Doug the Thug Ashur started bullying me, I tried to think of why. Because my hair was combed? Really? Because my shirts were ironed?

"You never know," said Candace. "Why don't you try wearing the same black Thor T-shirt five days a week like he does? Maybe you and Dougal could become best friends?"

I shuddered at the thought.

ONE THING I wouldn't do was tell anyone — any adult.

My parents were cool; we talked all the time. But if I had told them about Doug the Thug, they'd have gone into action mode. They'd have wanted me to go talk to the principal — or worse still, they'd have talked to her themselves. And that would have been disastrous. It would have been all that Doug needed to rearrange my nose, maybe break a few bones. No thanks, Mom and Dad.

All over the school there were posters saying stuff like, "Our Class is a No Bullying Zone" or "Step Up So Others Don't Get Stepped On" or "It Isn't Big to Make Others Feel Small." Even with all that, I couldn't imagine going up to Dougal and suggesting we become pals.

Who were those posters for, anyway? Were bullies expected to see them and have a change of heart? Did it make the administration feel like they were doing something constructive? Was the wimp brigade supposed to be inspired to gang together, somehow, and put up a united front against the goon squad?

Anyway, school had become a bit of a war zone for me and the snow of that Sunday night wasn't enough to warrant a snow day.

"HEY, it's my favorite pansy." Doug the Thug was waiting at the school door when I got off the bus. "Is that a yellow shirt? Didn't you get the memo?" he said. "Yellow is for fruit loops."

I had been talking to Candace on the bus. Doug swung the door open for her, bowing like a doorman as she went through, then slammed it shut in my face. "Not so fast, gear box."

I did a spin move worthy of Steph Curry and headed for the other door, but Doug ducked through the one he'd slammed in my face, met me on the other side and with his chest plowed me into the wall.

"Ashur, cool it!" The bus monitor had seen Doug corner me. "Now!" he said and with one last shove, Doug pulled away, scowling.

"Pussy," he said.

"Meow," I said and earned myself a punch in the shoulder the monitor never saw. I rubbed it while Dougal walked backward down the hall, a finger wagging at me. Don't mess with me, said the finger.

Ah, Monday.

MAYBE THOSE posters do work, sort of. That week Doug the Thug got caught a couple of times for giving me a rough time. In recess a couple of students "stepped up" and reported him for giving me a face wash in the snow. Friday he even got called out of class for pinning me to the wall in the locker room.

But here's where the whole anti-bullying crusade falls apart. It became pretty obvious that Doug's bad week of terrorizing was only going to turn into a way badder week for me. Revenge! Every time he got nabbed, he got more frustrated. Any warning he was given turned into a threat aimed at me, as if I was responsible for all the trouble he was getting into. Every caution upped the ante in his sick mind.

"He's not sick," said Candace. "I think he's just lonely."

"Well, if you think he's so lonely, why don't you be his friend?"

She screwed up her nose. "Not my type," she said. ·

153

"He's sure not mine," I said.

Friday afternoon, when I thought I was home free, he got in one last assault. He cornered me in the washroom, backed me into the wall, his face right up close to mine. "You do not want to make trouble for me," he said.

"You're right," I said. "I don't."

"Don't be a smart-ass."

He pressed his forehead against mine, forcing my skull back against the tiles. His eyes drilled into my eyes. I could smell his breath and it's not like it was bad, there was just way too much of it, as if he was getting near the end of some marathon. I turned away, my right cheek against the tiles. They were so cold. I closed my eyes, waiting for what was going to happen next. Steeling myself for the sucker punch, the knee to the groin, and all the time willing the door to open and for some brave kid to come in and shout, "Hey, it isn't big to make others feel small!"

Then he suddenly pulled away, swearing under his breath, and left, shaking his head, his hands deep in his pockets. As the door closed after him, I thought I heard him growl with exasperation, as if I just didn't get it.

And here's the truth: I just didn't get it.

Jack

I didn't move for a full minute. I'd never been so frightened in my life. I had to figure this out but I didn't know how. There had been something in his glare that alarmed me more than anything else he'd ever done to me. The bruises, the abrasions, the knuckle rubs … I could handle all of that, but when he glared at me like that, it was as if he had backed me into a deep hole and I'd started falling.

A LOT of kids don't like Sunday evening because it means … well, I don't need to spell it out. After that week, I was already bemoaning Monday morning on Friday evening! Mom and Dad picked up on it. Each took a turn asking me what was up.

"The sky," I told Mom.

"And what else?" she said.

"Nothing. Just … nothing."

"Is there some problem at school?" Dad asked.

"Yeah," I said. "School."

"You're a straight-A student."

"Then maybe you should let me get back to my homework."

My parents weren't the type to push too far. Like I said, we talked all the time. If I didn't want to talk, they weren't going to force the matter. But after Dad left my room, I didn't get back to my homework. I kept waiting for them to come storming back into the room and demand to know what was eating me. Pin me to the wall and exact a confession from me. I sat there at my desk and felt myself falling deeper and deeper into that hole Dougal Ashur had pushed me into.

Saturday night, I even dreamed of falling down into darkness. The entrance to the hole above me grew smaller and smaller until it was no more than a pinprick of light as distant as a star.

OLD MAN Sunday called.

"It's for you," said Mom, holding out the phone.

"Hello?"

"You busy?" he said.

"Not particularly."

"Then whyn't you come on over?"

I didn't have time to answer before he hung up.

"Maybe he needs his walk shoveled," said Mom.

There'd been another big snowfall that night and my tracks were the first ones in our drive-way. The road had been plowed and was grit-ty with sand, so it wasn't hard going and it felt good outside, the air clear and fresh. I breathed deeply, wanting that cold air to swirl away the remnants of my bad dream. The sky screamed blue.

Sunday's walk didn't need shoveling.

I knocked on his workshop door.

"When was it ever locked?" he shouted from inside.

I walked into the warmth of his old woodstove. He was working on a cabinet, which was going to have a mirror, and the sides to hold up that mirror were two blue herons facing one another. They weren't blue yet, just the warm, yellowy-brown of butternut, but you could almost see the color of the birds, the feathers were so alive.

He turned from where he was chiseling with something as fine as a surgeon's scalpel. "You made good time," he said.

I shrugged.

Then he put down his tool and made his way slowly, back bent a bit, across the shop to a work table. "Come and have a look," he said.

There on a piece of velvet stood a tiny perfect ermine. He was on his hind paws, his head gazing back over his shoulder; his tail curving around his body seemed to flicker with life. He wasn't any bigger than the palm of my hand, and when I picked him up, he sat there gazing up at me — smart and ready for anything.

"Seemed a shame to paint him," said Sunday. I nodded, feeling the smoothness of the wood with my finger. "So he's both animals at once," he said. "A stoat and an ermine."

"Right," I said. And then I thought how the real animal would still be the same whatever he looked like on the outside. I smiled. "He's amazing," I said. "You did it again: brought some dead critter back to life."

He laughed. "Nonsense," he said, swatting away my compliment as if it was a pesky fly.

I put the ermine down gently on the little square of velvet.

"It's yours," he said. I looked at him. "Seriously," he said. "Take it. Give it a good home." I'd undone my winter coat when I came in and Sunday picked up the carving and placed it in the breast pocket of my shirt. Turned it so that he faced out. I patted my pocket.

"Hi, Jack," I said.

Sunday smiled. "It's good to have a second set of eyes," he said.

THAT NIGHT I placed the ermine on the corner of my desk right near the head of my bed. Every now and then I'd reach out and poke my phone on so that I could see him there in the light, my Jack ermine. In the shadows he looked even realer, somehow, like he had just turned his head to look at me and wasn't frozen but only standing perfectly still so as not to give himself away.

When I fell asleep, I dreamed of a real ermine. I dreamed of him full of life again, and climbing back out of that coffin of a garbage pail. I watched him push his head up through the hole in the lid and then squirm with all his might right out the top of that pail and then take off into the wintry night, bounding across the snow, losing himself in the moonlit whiteness.

I TOOK the ermine to school with me. I wanted to show Candace. She loved it so much I almost wanted to give it to her. It would have been nice to see her smile. But I wasn't ready for that kind of stuff. I wanted Jack all to myself. For now, at least.

I showed it to some kids in my homeroom. "Your animal amigo," said Ms. Vermette, our homeroom teacher. I liked that. The ermine alive again.

AND THEN Dougal tracked me down.

"Let's see your pet weasel," he said.

I swung around. He was standing six feet off, rocking on his heels, his hands hanging easy by his sides.

How did he do it? How did he always know where I was?

"Word's out, Mr. Clean. Show me." The ermine was alert in my breast pocket, its head peeking over the rim, looking directly at him. "Is that it?" said Dougal. He scoffed. "Sure is small."

"Stop stalking me," I said.

For some reason the words affected him. I watched the expression on his face crack, saw him cross his arms defensively across his chest.

"I'm not stalking you," he said.

"Yes, you are."

"You wish."

"No, I don't wish. And you are stalking me. That's what this is." He tightened the grip of his arms and his face seemed to wince as if he'd been hit. *Don't back away*, the ermine whispered to me.

"What do you want from me?" I shouted.

He dropped his arms. "I don't want —"

"What?" I said, again.

"I don't … I can't …"

And it was then, with him not able to explain it, that suddenly I could, sort of. More from the tortured look on his face than from anything he could bring himself to say.

"Oh," I said.

I took a deep breath. And we stood like that, the distance between us being about as long as his shadow. *Go,* Jack ermine whispered to me. *Leave, but don't run.*

I didn't run. I walked right past Dougal Ashur, close enough he could have shoulder-checked me, but I was counting on him not doing it. He didn't.

I was the length of my shadow past him when he spoke again.

"I like you," he said, so quiet no one could have heard it but me if there'd been anyone around.

I stopped and turned. He hadn't turned; he was still facing the wall where he'd trapped me.

"You sure have a weird way of showing it."

"I can't … I don't want …"

I sighed. "You said that already."

He turned around now, very slowly, and I expected to see anger on his face. I was being a smart-ass and he didn't like that. But there wasn't anger there.

"Don't make fun of me," he said.

I threw up my arms. "You make fun of me all the time. You treat me like —"

"I know. I know. I'm sorry," he said. "Really."

He was struggling with something. Something big. He liked me and he had no idea what to do with that. Neither did I. But I had my ermine sitting boldly in my pocket, alert, watching, quick, ready. Giving me strength.

Show him, Jack whispered.

"It's not a weasel," I said.

"What?"

I patted my chest pocket. "And it's not a pet."

He stared at my chest and then at my face. He nodded.

I reached up and took the ermine out and held it out to him. He took it tentatively and looked it over, his eyes fixated on it. And his finger did what mine had done, when Old Man Sunday showed it to me, felt the curve and grace of it, the life of it. Gradually, Dougal's out-of-control breathing returned to normal. And then, reluctantly, he handed it back.

I put it in my pocket, patted it. It was then I noticed that the anti-bullying brigade had made it to this farthest corner of the school. There was a poster on the wall: "Be a Buddy, Not a Bully." Beside the first phrase, there was a big red thumbs-up, and beside the second, a big red thumbs-down.

"Did you see that?" I said, nodding toward the poster. Dougal glanced at it and then turned back to me. He didn't do anything, he still seemed sort of frozen. So it was up to me, I guess.

I gave him a thumbs-up.

Hesitantly, he gave me a thumbs-up. I'm not sure this meant we were buddies, but it was all I could think of to do. With one last look, I turned to go. Then I stopped and turned toward him, again.

"Are we good?" I said.

THE STUFFED TOY

THERE IS a den at the back of Robin's house where a bear lives. A very old, crusty bear, with yellowing teeth and liver spots on his wrinkly paws. The bear has a name, although he doesn't always respond to it on account of his ears. They're clogged up with hair.

"Eh?" he says.

Then you have to shout, "Good morning, Gramps!"

And then you have to wait to see who will answer, the old man or the bear.

The old man will likely smile a crinkly smile at you and say, "Why, good morning, Mistress

Robin." He might ask you for tea and, if you're not going to school that day, you might stay, because he has a teapot with a cozy on it and white cups in white saucers, each with thin rings of gold and blue around the edge, and he serves English tea biscuits — not cookies — that are covered with sugar or coated with chocolate or filled with fruit cream.

If you're having one of those days where you feel like you're in a suspense movie, then tea with a chocolate-coated digestive biscuit can sometimes keep the dread at bay. You can look out at the woods behind the house through Gramps's picture window and say to yourself, those are just woods. That movement in the leaves is just the wind.

There are no leaves now. It's the dead of winter, when there's no sun to charge your batteries and the dread feels near at hand. Hovering.

Sometimes, when you say, "Good morning, Gramps," the bear answers you.

"Gramps? What kind of a foolish name is that?" grumps the bear. "I'll tell you summit, child, I'm not your gramps, I'm your *great*-grandfather and a foolish handle that is if I ever heard one. I outlived my wife and then I bloody well outlived both my son and daughter — what's so 'great' about that, I ask you?"

The Stuffed Toy

Except he isn't asking you, so don't dare answer. He's in a "foul" mood, as he'll tell you if you hang around long enough to hear. And sometimes Robin does because it's kind of exhilarating to watch his eyes grow all big and roll around in their yellow-tinged sockets, while his bushy eyebrows rise high on his crinkly forehead and his whole body stiffens as if maybe he's in a suspense movie, too, and has no idea what's going to happen next.

Robin is named Robin after her grandfather, who died before she really knew him. Gramps was already ninety-one when his son died. He's one hundred now and she's the only Robin he has left.

She figures he's allowed to be a bear now and then.

You want to be careful, when you knock on his door. And Robin, being Robin, is always careful. She worries — worries, sometimes, that it won't be either Gramps or the bear who is there, but only a century-old body lying in the bed Gramps used to sleep in.

TODAY, no one answers and Robin fears the worst. She knocks again. Still no answer. Except, when she presses her ear to the wooden door, there's someone talking with an English accent that's nothing like Gramps's East Sussex dialect. It's the BBC. Tentatively, she opens the door. The TV is on, but Gramps's favorite chair is empty. He's nowhere to be seen, but the closet door is open and suddenly a black coat comes flying out like a witch taking off, followed by an umbrella and a suitcase.

"Gramps?"

He pokes his head out. "Ah, Robin," he says. "The very girl I was hoping for." Then he heads back into the closet and more things fly out: a walking stick, a tweed jacket, a hot water bottle.

"What are you looking for?" Robin asks from a safe distance.

He steps out and scratches his head, as if he's forgotten. But he hasn't; it just takes him a moment, sometimes. "The stuffed toy," he says. "You know the one." She doesn't. Then he scratches his head again. "Only, I'm quite sure Dulcie gave it to Susan." He shakes his head. "What was she thinking on to go and do that?" he says, quite bewildered by the thought.

Dulcie was Gramps's wife and Susan was their daughter, Robin's great-aunt. Robin knows these people only as old black-and-white photographs of people standing very still and straight, wearing slightly frightened smiles in case they blinked and ruined the picture.

"Well?" he says.

"I don't know, Gramps," says Robin. "A stuffed toy?"

"It's middling strange," he says standing there framed in the closet doorway. Then all the oomph goes out of him and he sags so much that his suspenders threaten to slip right off his narrow shoulders. She goes to him then and sits him down in his favorite chair in front of the television.

She stands at his side, patting his shoulder, watching soccer results on the screen. Except Gramps calls it football and he likes Brighton & Hove Albion who are in sixteenth place but won't be relegated, he's explained to her, although she's uncertain what being relegated means. He's not watching the scores right now. His eyes have gone all big and he's in his suspense thriller again. Robin has sometimes wondered if the unseen danger in his movie is the same as the unseen danger in hers. It's impossible to know.

"It was the forest fire made me think on it," he says.

She looks out the window in case there's a forest fire she didn't know about. But it's February outside and there's nothing brighter than snow out there.

"What fire, Gramps?"

"Why, the Ashdown Forest," he says. "It was right there, on the telly. In Nutley, not five miles as the crow flies from Hartfield. You know, Robin." He stares at Robin as if all of this should make sense — as if she were his son, Robin, who died years ago, not his great-granddaughter.

Only one thing he says means anything to her: the Ashdown Forest. It's where A. A. Milne, author of the Winnie-the-Pooh books, lived, and where Christopher Robin played. Gramps's son was named after that Robin, so she guesses she was, too, in a twice-removed kind of way.

Gramps and Dulcie grew up on the edge of the Ashdown Forest, way back when.

Robin's hand has been resting on Gramps's shoulder and now he reaches up with his big old spotty paw and pats it.

"Poor little soul," he says.

"I'm okay, Gramps."

"No, I mean the stuffed toy. Whatever will Susan have done with it, that scatterbrained lass?"

The weather comes on the BBC. Oh, the presenter only has one arm! Robin leans on the back of her great-grandfather's chair and watches. One arm is enough, it seems, for pointing out weather patterns, especially in a country as small as the United Kingdom. How strange it would be, she thinks, to live in a country where everyone experienced pretty much the same weather on any given day.

The whole country is having record-high temperatures for this time of the year, the presenter says. February is bursting into flames all over.

"Poor wee thing," says Gramps, shaking his head again as if it was really the fire, not Susan, that was the stuffed toy's problem. "I fear the worst," he says, patting Robin's hand again.

That's the thing that joins Robin and her great-granddad together. They both fear the worst.

ROBIN CHECKS with her father. He doesn't recall anything about a stuffed toy, but he knows all about his aunt Susan. "She never stayed still, always flying off somewhere or other. Just couldn't settle. Not someone you'd leave anything of value to, unless it was money."

But because she knows her parents well, Robin also checks with her mother.

"Ah, Aunt Susan," she says. "What a marvelous woman. Traveled the world, never married."

"Is there something you're not telling me, Mom?"

Robin's mother laughs gayly and twitches Robin's nose. "You're my world," she says. "I wouldn't change you for anything."

"Or go away?"

"Or ever, ever go away."

"So the stuffed toy …"

Her mother shrugs. "Don't know about that, but Susan left all her earthly possessions here. Out in the barn."

The barn. Robin shudders.

THAT NIGHT Gramps calls out in his sleep and as the only other person awake in the vast sleeping farmhouse, Robin goes to him.

"I'll find it, Dulcie," says Gramps. "Have no fear of that. I'll get him to safety, luv."

Robin pats his shoulder and says, "Shhh, it's all right, Gramps," which takes an act of courage on her part because it's dark in Gramps's flat, but for stray bits of moonlight. "Shhh," she says again, and this time it's for herself, too. *Pat, pat, pat.* And Gramps lies there, his mouth open, breathing hard, looking up at the ceiling through eyes that are open and unseeing.

"Poor little soul," he says. "Poor wee thing."

Gradually, his breathing softens and his eyes close and he drifts back to whatever corner of the world of sleep he can get to on his tired old legs. And Robin is pleased with herself, for it was often Gramps who would come to quiet her back to sleep when she was little and had only just become aware of the Bad Thing.

"Is it the Bad Thing?" he'd ask.

And she'd nod.

"Ah, well," he'd say. "I'll keep an eye out for it, lass. You sleep, now. I'll stand watch."

She would train her eyes on his tall, lank silhouette against the light from her mostly closed door, while he stood not two feet away from her bedside, his back to her, his hands lightly clenched behind him, like a guard at ease, but vigilant, his head scanning every corner of the room. Eventually she'd sleep.

So now, Robin stands watch. And when Gramps is truly asleep, she wanders over to his window and looks out through her own breath on the frosted glass at the moon peeking through scudding clouds, and the tree shadows and the shadow of the wood smoke writing on the clean white sheets of snow. And lurking off to her left across the yard, the ramshackle old barn.

—

"Do you think he's losing his mind?" she asks her father.

"Not your great-grandfather," he says. "Got a mind like a steel trap."

"What does that mean?"

"Like the door on an animal trap that snaps shut," says her father. He snaps his hand together as if catching something in midair. Robin wonders about that, about ideas caught like that, trapped.

For a second night, the old man dreams of the stuffed toy and Robin goes to him. She tells her mother in the morning, who says, "Well, he does have a steel-trap mind, but the hinges need a little oil now and then." She hands Robin some worksheets of exponents and square roots, and Robin sits to do them at the kitchen island, still in her pajamas, a plate of toast and honey at her side. She doesn't complain. This is the trade-off: stay home from school, you get a lot of homework.

"He gets befuddled," says her mother after a while.

When Robin's done her math and has read two chapters of *Harry Potter à l'école des sorciers*, she decides to go and see how Gramps is doing. Only, when she knocks, the bear answers.

"Not in," he says in a growly voice.

"Gramps, it's me."

"Nobody here," he says.

"Gramps?"

"I heard you quite well the first time," he says.

She turns to go, then stops and smiles to herself. It's a line from *Winnie-the-Pooh*. Rabbit's line, when Pooh comes to visit … A mind like a steel trap, she thinks.

But when she knocks again, he's still growly. She goes in anyway and sees him looking out at the snowy landscape, stretching out his bony fingers and folding them back into gnarly fists.

"I think the stuffed toy is safe," she says, to see if that helps ease his mind. It doesn't. He's got a sour look on his face and his eyes are very far away. She can almost see the fire in them. He's somewhere on the other side of the Atlantic, looking out at a fire raging in the Ashdown Forest, where he and Dulcie used to play when they were children.

"They put the fires out, Gramps," she says. "Didn't you see it on the news?"

He doesn't answer her. His eyes are big with worry. She reaches out to pat his arm, then draws it back and leaves. But before she makes it to the door, he mutters something under his breath.

"She should never have taken the blasted thing," he says, or at least that's what she thinks she hears.

"What's that, Gramps?" she says in her careful-lest voice.

"Given us no end of trouble," he mumbles.

HER MOTHER makes her go out, even though it's gray and dismal and Februaryish.

"Just because we're doing homeschool doesn't mean I have to have recess," Robin says.

"No, but you need some air," says her mother, "and I need a break."

Robin stands outside in the dismal yard in the soggy air and looks over at the old barn. A piece of its loose tin roof flaps in the breeze. *Slap. Slap.* Robin shivers and digs her hands deep into her coat pockets. If it were a bright sunshiny day, she might just risk it. The place is structurally sound, even if it is dilapidated. There are spaces between the wood siding so that there are bands of light inside. She remembers thinking of them as music when she was little.

She could leave the big door open. If she

could find the stuffed toy, maybe it would cheer Gramps up, snap him out of his grumpiness. But the problem is, Great-Aunt Susan's stuff is in the room *inside* the barn. The room Dad built as a recording studio, but never got around to actually using, except for storage. There are no windows in that room. There's a low roof. And insulation so that no sound can come in or out. If she were trapped there, no one would ever know. And anyway, there'd be no guarantee that she'd find anything. What stuffed toy?

She should never have taken the blasted thing. That's what Gramps had said.

Taken it? Like, stolen it?

Given us no end of trouble.

Robin shivers and it's not just the bone-deep, wet cold of the weather. She looks around the yard. It looks so lonesome. And the dread seeps in: a tightening in the chest, panic, despair.

Her brain thermostat is miss-set. It was something she'd overheard Mom say to her father.

Is it like that for Gramps? They never talk about it. She just sees in his eyes what she imagines someone sees in hers, when the suspense movie starts rolling.

She raps on the kitchen door. "Am I allowed back in yet?" she says.

"Oh, don't be silly," says her mother.

"IT'S JUST a phase."

She hears them talking when they think she's asleep.

"It's a gateway disorder," says Mom. "We need to think about seeing someone."

"She's on the brink of her teens — the biggest disorder of all. Everybody goes through that."

"I feel like I'm in 'fix-it mode,'" says Mom.

"She'll be fine. She's great," says Dad.

"I didn't say she wasn't."

"She just needs to pull herself up by her boot-straps."

Outside their bedroom door, Robin looks down at her slippers. No bootstraps there. Just as well. If you pulled yourself up by your bootstraps, wouldn't you just fall over?

She shakes her head. It's nothing she hasn't overheard before. She overhears a lot. And she's mostly okay and then she's not. Especially at this time of the year. There's a girl at school, Wanda, who came up to her once, out of the blue, and said quietly, so no one else would hear, "Me too, *chica*."

The Stuffed Toy

Robin must have looked confused, because Wanda held out her T-shirt for Robin to see. There was Dorothy from *The Wizard of Oz* with her hand up to her open mouth and her eyes wide with panic. Maybe it was the moment when the Wicked Witch stole her dog.

"It gets scary," said Wanda. "The anxiety, right?" Robin nodded. "Especially in the winter." Robin nodded again. They didn't talk much but it was good to know she had an ally.

She pads softly down the hall from her parents' room and listens at Gramps's door. The BBC is on very low. But if she listens she can hear him talking, as if he were on the phone, except that he's talking to Dulcie.

"I know, Dulcie, I know," he says. "Yes, luv. But it's like gawm on your boots. You can't shake it off and it reeks, it does."

Robin wonders what gawm is. Mud of some kind, probably. Gramps has a hundred words for mud. She imagines Sussex must be wall to wall mud, considering how many words there are for it. And here he is talking to his wife about it — Dulcie who died not long after Robin was born. She wonders if gawm is the kind of mud that can foul up a steel-trap mind and make an old man go screwball.

—

ROBIN DREAMS of fire. She's trapped in a cardboard box in a barn of dry old wood that would burn up like tinder. She wakes to a day of brittle sunshine that disappears by the time she's showered.

"School today?" says Dad, hopeful as ever.

"Not yet," she says.

"I'll give you a drive, save you having to take the yellow peril?"

"Thanks, Dad, but no. I've got plans."

"But, Rob —"

"Honey," says Mom in the tone of voice that's reserved for Dad when he's going on the offensive. Robin gives him a quick hug and then ducks under his arm and down the hall.

"Plans?" he calls after her.

She nods without turning and slips into her bedroom. She does have plans. She wasn't lying. She leans back against the door, as if expecting Dad to force his way in for a little heart-to-heart about bootstraps. But he doesn't come. Still she leans against the door, not to keep anything out but because she's afraid of what she's going to do. She tries to talk herself out of it, loses, and then stands up tall and only a bit wobbly. She'll need some things.

"Where are you going with that bat?" says her

mother. Robin was hoping to get out unseen. "I thought we were going to be looking at British North America after the fall of New France."

If there was ever a good reason to do something daring, there it was.

"We will, Mom. I promise. Can't wait. But there's something I've got to do first. It's important."

Hands on hips, her mother looks her over, from her headlamp down to her sturdy boots.

"The whistle's in case you run into problems?" Robin nods. "If the bat isn't enough?" Robin nods again. Now her mother nods. "Do you want me to …"

Go with me? Yes! No!

"Okay," says Mom.

And so Robin goes.

SHE FORCES the barn door open as far as she can, which isn't that far on account of the snow. She holds it open with a sawhorse that's standing just inside the door. There's her father's MG that he's been fixing up for six years. The tarp covering it is dusty and covered with bird droppings. There are old beehives in the corner, another failed project. The bears got more honey than the humans did. The barn is where hobbies go to die.

Birds live there. Mice, too. Probably rats, though she's never seen one. She grips her bat tight, and steps inside, makes her way down past the stalls, where cows were mangered when this was a working farm, a long time ago. There's nothing left of them but the sweet, dry smell. She breathes in deeply and ends up sneezing her head off. Dust. The place is alive with dust. The bands of light that penetrate the gloom are thick with it.

There's a heavy wooden gate at the end of the stalls, tied shut with a length of binder twine. She opens it, steps through and closes it behind her. Then she takes a right and a left and the light of the outside fades to nothing. She flips on her headlamp and immediately wishes she hadn't. There was that movie — a real one — she hadn't meant to see, but she was with friends and they all watched it and she's never liked to see anything by flashlight beam since, except the pages of her book when she's reading late, safe in bed.

She turns around, her bat ready. Nothing stirs but the wind. The barn grumbles. A loose board rattles, the tin roof goes slap, slap. The wind dies. Ahead of her is the door to the recording studio. There's a sign on it that says, "Quiet, please: Recording in progress."

The Stuffed Toy

She opens the door. There is a deeper, thicker kind of darkness inside. There are no windows, no way out if the door should slam shut behind her and jam, somehow. Or if someone were to lock her in and her headlamp battery died and she fell and tore her leg on a nail and the already low roof started to lower and her voice clogged up with dust so that she couldn't blow on her whistle.

Robin takes a deep breath and is glad she can. The air is cooler in here. A tomb, she thinks, and immediately regrets it. "Get a grip," she tells herself. Which isn't the same as picking yourself up by your bootstraps.

You came to rescue a stuffed toy.

No. To rescue your Gramps.

There, isn't that better? She takes another deep breath and finally lets go of the door handle, though she holds her foot against it until she's maneuvered a heavy box of what she suspects are books into the door's path.

There are many boxes. Too many boxes. Not just Great-Aunt Susan's, either. Boxes of their stuff, too. And old furniture. She turns and looks back where she came. She could march out of here right now and just say she couldn't find it. And Mom would say, how about we look again after lunch, I'll help. And so they'd do some history and eat some lunch and come out here and she'd stand there while her mother moved boxes around and found the damned stuffed toy, which, after all, was the only reason she was doing this and maybe there wasn't even a damned stuffed toy.

A damned stuffed toy.

She should never have taken the blasted thing. Again, Gramps's words come back to her

The movie starts to roll. She can hear the Cellos of the Damned start to murmur. It'll be the Violins of the Damned next. She looks at the stacks of boxes. What was that saying? A journey of a thousand miles starts with a single step? "Replace step with box," Robin tells herself out loud, trying to drown out the film score. With one last fleeting and longing look back to make sure the door to this inner chamber is really going to stay open, she launches in.

She's not sure how long it is — ten hours or fifteen minutes — before she finds the Susan cache. There's a big red *SUSAN* on every box. And there are only a couple of dozen boxes. Robin is sweaty and cold at the same time.

Then she opens one box and screams and steps backward and tumbles over on her backside. She takes a moment to gather her courage. By then she knows whose eyes they are and she gets shakily to her knees. Dolls. Robin leans one hand on the cold wall and rests the other on her heart. This is prime horror-story stuff. Dolls. Very old dolls, by the look of them. Susan's dolls? Maybe even Great-Grandmother Dulcie's dolls. Porcelain and cloth and wood, in stained white nighties and dresses with tattered, frilly collars. When she's re-covered, she starts to unpack the dolls very carefully, afraid they might fall apart in her hands. One by one, she places them on the floor around her.

And then, suddenly, there it is.

Has to be.

She had no idea what she was looking for, but this must be it. She picks it up lovingly and places it in the palm of her hand. It's baby Roo. Kanga's son. One eye is hanging by a thread. His pelt is threadbare. Still, she'd recognize him anywhere. She rests the stuffed doll on a spare piece of tissue paper one of the other dolls had been wrapped in and then, just to be 100 percent sure, she looks through the rest of the box. But there are no more characters from Winnie-the-Pooh. Just this.

Filled with excitement and desperate to go — but reminding herself to be gentle — she packs away all the other dolls and then picks up Roo and cradles him in one arm. He's very small and fragile. She gets to her feet and leaves the dark room, slowly, carefully, afraid she might damage him. He could tear in an instant, she thinks. She imagines him disintegrating like a dandelion clock. She closes the door to the studio and heads out. She's already out the barn door before she remembers that she left her bat in the studio. She doesn't need it, she tells herself, and then she makes herself go back for it. Just because she can.

"OH, GOD. Of course!" says Mom. She's delicately balancing baby Roo on the palm of her hand, with the other hand cupped nearby in case he should decide to sproing off her hand onto the kitchen counter.

"What do you mean, 'of course'?"

Mom shakes her head. "The fires in the Ashdown Forest. That's where they found him. No wonder he's so upset." Robin is about to burst. "Let him explain," her mother says and hands the tiny kangaroo back to Robin.

As she's leaving the room, her mother calls out to her. "That was brave, Rob," she says.

Robin frowns, feels foolish. "Not really."

"Was, too. You did something hard. Did it alone."

"The barn's just … just spooky." That's all. It's only a place, a thing. What's really scary is the unexpected. Things that come out of nowhere …

What's really scary is what isn't anything.

SHE KNOCKS on Gramps's door.

"I'm still not in," says the bear. "Not to meddling little misses. Now, leave an old man in peace."

"No," says Robin. Then, not waiting for the bear to argue, she goes in. He's sitting by the window looking out at the bleakness of late winter. "Look what I found," she says.

He takes little Roo in his old hands, which are shaking. Oh, he stares at it. Stares in wonder as if seeing it for the first time. He looks at her and she sees that his eyes are wet. Then he looks out at the cold leafless forest and then back at Roo.

Robin is bursting with questions but she holds them at bay, leaves him the space for his steel-trap mind to digest what she has placed in his hands. After a moment, she turns and finds the hassock that sits in front of his favorite chair, drags it over to the window and plunks down on it beside him.

There. Now she can wait as long as it takes. And after several trillion seconds, he tells her a story.

They were kiddies together, he and Dulcie. Next-door neighbors in Hartfield, Sussex. They did everything together and they played in the Ashdown Forest, never knowing that it would become famous the world over as the "100 Aker Wood."

"Christopher Robin was our age. We saw him sometimes, he and his nurse, when the family was down from London. Never really knew the boy. Had no idea his dad was a famous playwright up in't city. Didn't know about the Pooh books. Not 'til much later. By then ... well, it was too late."

He blinks a tear from his eye, takes a huge white handkerchief from his pocket and wipes it away. Robin's Gramps is never without his handkerchief. When she was little she took one of them to show-and-tell. She explained what it was and showed the class the blue initials stitched into the corner.

"What do you mean, 'too late'?" she says.

"Too late to return it, of course."

Robin stares at Roo. "You stole it?"

Gramps doesn't answer right away. "It weren't like that," he says. "We found it. Found it sitting in the crotch of an old apple tree. We were out exploring, as children do, and there it was. There was no one around. Made it seem as if the wee thing had jumped up into the tree all by itself. How were we to know?"

He turns to Robin and she can only shrug. "So you took it?"

"Dulcie did. I was uneasy about it, but then I was always uneasy, like. Dulcie was the plucky one. Got us into scrapes, she did." He smiles. "I think it wasn't until I was more your sort of age that I ever saw the books. *Winnie-the-Pooh* and t'others. And there were Mr. Shepard's drawings. What a fright that was. There was Roo and there was Dulcie's stuffed Roo and they were one and the same."

"But how do you know it was Christopher Robin's toy? I mean, there could have been lots of them."

"Which is just what I said to Dulcie, she was that upset."

Robin is perplexed and it must show on her face because Gramps pats her on the arm and, having handed Roo back to her, laboriously climbs out of his chair and goes to his bookshelf. He pulls out a slim volume and returns to her. His fingers are not shaking anymore as he opens the book and turns the pages. "Here it is," he says, and hands it to her.

With her thumb holding the place, she closes the book to look at the cover. *The Enchanted Places* by Christopher Milne. Oh! Then she looks at the page Gramps has found and reads it, a passage about Christopher — *the* Christopher Robin — walking out with his nanny and leaving Roo in the crotch of an apple tree, only to find it gone when he returned.

"Oh!" says Robin again.

"It was so many years later. We were in our fifties, by then. And Dulcie … well, she wouldn't — couldn't let it go."

Robin stares at the small stuffed toy. "It's probably worth a lot," she says.

Gramps nods his head in agreement. "Which is why I feared for it when I saw the fires in the Ashford Forest."

"But it was —"

"I know, child." Gramps tapped his head. "It's just sometimes I don't know what I know."

"Your steel-trap mind needs oiling," she says.

And Gramps laughs and nods again. He stares at her, his forehead wrinkling. He reaches out and taps the lens of her headlamp with his fingernail. "What's this about?" he asks.

"I had to go somewhere dark to get Roo," she says.

"And how was that?" he asks.

"Worth it," she says.

THE BROTHERHOOD OF
INTERSTELLAR DIRT

I WAS at the bedroom window when Dad came in. The window was open and the crickets were going wild, as if maybe they knew what was coming.

"How's Mom?" I asked, keeping my voice quiet.

He waffled his hand in a so-so gesture, which I could see in the light spilling in from the hall. Then he closed the door behind him and it was dark again, except for the stars. He joined me at the window.

"Any sightings?" Dad asked.

"Not yet. Too early."

"It's after eleven."

"Oh, that's right, I forgot, I've got school tomorrow. Oh, wait. It's August, no I don't."

Dad smiled a careworn smile as he craned his eyes up. "Sky's clear. What's the forecast for tomorrow?"

"No rain. No clouds. The moon will set by 8:47, so it'll be good and dark. Perfect."

Dad didn't say anything, but he had something to say. I could tell even by starlight.

"Is she really okay?" I asked.

"She's fine," he said.

"Spill it, Dad."

"Okay. She's having mild contractions."

"But she's not due for another week, right?"

"Yeah, well. Contractions of thirty to forty seconds, every ten minutes or so, say different."

I lurched a bit inside. "So, that's good, isn't it? The sooner the better?"

"Well, yeah. Except for one thing: your party."

"What about it?"

"There's a pretty good chance your mom will be giving birth by tomorrow."

"So?" I said. "It's only Artie, Ope and Ricardo."

"I know. But we might not even be here, Mom and I."

I cross my arms on the windowsill and lean my forehead on the glass.

"Noah, I'm just not sure their parents will like us leaving you guys alone."

"We're not going to raid the liquor cabinet, if that's what you're worried about."

"I'm not worried about that."

"Oh, right. Drugs. I forgot. Yeah, well, Ric was going to score some spice from his big brother. Or maybe some bath salts."

"Bath salts?"

"Synthetic cathinones: gotta keep up, Dad."

He sighed and leaned his head on the glass, too. He didn't say anything, but it was as if the glass was transmitting his thoughts, forehead to forehead. He was going to leave it to me to give in — do the right thing. I was pretty reliable that way, but not this time.

"Father," I said, wanting to add a little tone to my objection, "have you ever met a nerdier group of twelve-year-olds than Artie, Ope, Ricardo and me?" I glanced sideways. His eyes were closed but he was smiling. "Think about it. They're coming over to watch the Perseid Shower. We're going to lie out on the back lawn in our sleeping bags, counting meteoroids as they burn up in the Earth's atmosphere. It's the closest any of us get to a sporting event. We're going to eat too many

Doritos — the original, unflavored kind — and drink too much Dr. Pepper — you know, counteract the heavy salt intake with a really high sugar intake. That's about the extent of the trouble we'll get into. We might forget to brush our teeth."

"Okay, okay, I hear you," said Dad. He sounded weary. I didn't want to fight with him, but this was a big deal. I was the last of the four dweeb-amigos to turn twelve.

"This is the last birthday before I become a teenager. Next year, who knows what I'll be up to? But you've got to trust me now."

"I do trust you, Noah. I trust all of you. I'm only saying their folks may not approve of us taking off in the middle of the evening. We might already be gone when the guys arrive."

"So, lets phone them first thing tomorrow," I said. "Let them know what's up. See what they say. Does that sound fair?"

Dad pushed back from the sill. "Yep," he said, but then he was distracted by a flash outside. Me, too. A shooting star over the woods behind the house. "Nice," said Dad. He turned to go. Then we heard a noise and turned to the window again.

"It's just cars out on the highway," I said after listening a moment.

"Sounds closer," said Dad. He was frowning. "You wouldn't have left the gate unlocked in the back meadow, would you?"

"Nope. Haven't been out there for ages."

Dad nodded. "I'll talk to Charlie," he said.

Just then the sound of a vehicle revving high cut through the cricket sounds. Could have been an ATV, but it sounded like a car. Whatever it was, Dad was right, it was close, even though we couldn't see any headlights through the trees. He shook his head. Then he patted me on the shoulder and headed back to Mom.

I turned to the window again. The baby wasn't even born and he was already shaking things up. A mistake. The baby was a mistake.

"Not really," Mom had said. "Let's call it — him — a surprise." Him. A him who was on the way. Almost here. Whoa! He might even be born on my birthday! I rested my head against the glass again. *Next, he'll want my bedroom*, I thought. I closed my eyes and into the darkness roared the sound of racing cars.

There was definitely more than one vehicle tooling around. We had seventy-six acres of land. Most of it was bush, but there was old farmland out there that hadn't yet been completely taken over by juniper and prickly ash and baby pines. Our neighbor Charlie kept sheep out in our back meadow, which was fenced off. But there was an old train bed bordering the meadow that the telephone company kept up for the cable they buried there. People used the train bed as a trail for cross-country skiing or snowmobiling in the winter, and for ATVs in the summer.

But a chained gate was only a minor inconvenience to some of the yahoos in our neck of the woods. We once phoned in a stolen vehicle someone had parked behind the old run-down barn out in the meadow.

The vehicles stopped, first one, then another, then a third. If I strained my ears I could hear yelling, laughing, like maybe there was a drunken party out there. Maybe they'd gathered to watch the shower. Somehow, I doubted it.

The Perseid Shower is my special birthday present. It lasts a few days but it reaches its peak right on August the twelfth. Thank you, Comet 109P/Swift-Tuttle. That's where the meteors come from. Swift-Tuttle takes 133 years to orbit the sun, but every single year the Earth passes through its trail of debris, which is all that meteors are, really. Dirt.

When I was a little kid I really thought they were shooting stars, especially the fireballs — they're the ones that leave long wakes of luminous ionized matter. Ric said he used to call them glow worms, but whoever heard of a worm that traveled at sixty-five kilometers per second?

DAD PHONED the parents the next morning and they all said it was fine for the four of us to be alone. There was one moment of panic. Ope's mother suggested that his older sister could babysit us. But, according to Dad, as soon as she said it, a civil war erupted on the other end of the line. Mrs. Opeka got back on the phone and said, in a shaky voice, that it was okay for Justin to come alone.

"There's no way Ope would want Elsa to babysit," I said.

"She said she'd rather die," said Dad.

So everything was set. And as soon as everything was set, Mom went into serious labor, almost as if she'd been waiting. By four in the afternoon they were out the door and the house was mine. I watched them drive off, feeling nervous. They had so much stuff with them — bags and bags — as if they were moving away. I closed the door and leaned against it. We had been going to drive down to the Kennedy Space Center and catch a launch next spring. That wasn't going to happen, not anymore.

I shook it off. Got to work on the robotic arm building kit they'd got me for my birthday.

Time flies when you're building robotic arms and before I knew it the guys were arriving. The guys and the pizzas, courtesy of Artie's mom.

Artie got me an Optimus Prime wall decal.

"I tried to get him life-size but I couldn't find one," he said.

"Which is just as well," said Ope. "At 6.7 meters, he'd go up one wall, across your ceiling and come down the other wall."

Ope got me an Albert Einstein action figure. I took him out of his box. "Hmm, the elusive unified field theory," I said. I tried to make Einstein scratch his head but he wasn't that versatile. "Nope, can't figure it out." Then I had Einstein point his finger at Ope. "Guess you'll have to do it, Mr. Opeka."

But the best present was the last. Ricardo had made me a micrometeorite necklace just like his. Ric collects micrometeorites. This one was about the size of a pea. He'd fused it in glass in his microwave kiln. I put it on, and he pulled his out from under his shirt.

"Mine's bigger," he said and we all laughed.

"Yeah, well mine's the biggest," said Artie. Then he patted himself on the chest. "Oh, wait. I don't have a micrometeorite necklace."

"Yes, you do," said Ric, and then he pulled two more necklaces out of his pocket, one for Artie and one for Ope.

When we were all wearing our micrometeorite necklaces, I said, "That pretty well proves it."

"What?" said Ric.

"We are the totally flashest dweeb-amigos in the known universe."

WHEN YOU see a shooting star, it's the light caused by the friction on a piece of comet debris entering our atmosphere. It might only be the size of a piece of popcorn but it heats up so hot it vaporizes. Every now and then one actually lands — not all that often, although we keep hoping we'll find one.

Meanwhile *tons* of micrometeorites fall to Earth every single day. Space dust. Ric gets micros from his rain gutter. True! Here's how it works: rain washes all the crud that ends up on your roof into the gutter. If you filter out the leaves and twigs and other debris, and if you find something that looks like rock, chances are you've got yourself a micro. You can tell for sure if you put it under a microscope; it'll be rounded and pitted, a sign of its fiery trip through the atmosphere.

I looked at mine and thought about Mom's amber brooch. Amber is sap that fossilized and sometimes something gets trapped in it, like an insect. Mom's insect might be a million years old — maybe a hundred million years old. But a micrometeorite is a particle from the formation of the solar system and it's over four *billion* years old.

We're all just stardust, Mom likes to say.

"What's the matter?" said Ope. "You look stunned."

"He always looks stunned," said Artie, "Now, he looks like he's going to cry because he has the best friends in the world."

"The Brotherhood of Interstellar Dirt," I said. We all clinked are micro necklaces together, like a toast, and then stuffed them down our shirts. It's one thing knowing you're a first-class dork, but you don't have to go around advertising it.

WE FRITTERED the daylight away playing *Civilization 1*. Dad phoned and told me Mom was fine, but the baby was being stubborn.

"Guess he's happy where he is," said Dad.

"Okay," I said. Wasn't sure where to go with that.

"You guys cool?"

"Yeah, we're playing *Civ 1*."

"What happened to *Civ 6*?"

"We're feeling nostalgic. Anyway, it's hilarious. Gandhi keeps dropping nuclear bombs on people."

"Gandhi?"

"Yeah, it's a programming glitch."

"Okay," says Dad, sounding bewildered. "Uh ..."

"What?"

"Just a heads-up," said Dad. "If the baby holds out too much longer, they might have —"

"Yeah, I know. We talked about this," I said. About how much trouble Mom went through having me. About maybe needing to have a C-section.

"You there, Noah?"

"Yeah."

"Okay, just wanted to keep you in the picture. They're about to —"

"I gotta get back, Dad," I said, interrupting him. "It's my turn and I need to enhance my alliances before Gandhi nukes me. Give Mom a hug."

I hung up before he painted the picture any more vividly.

Finally, it was dark. Good and dark. No moon. We placed our sleeping bags pointing in the four cardinal directions and lay down with our heads together at the center, like we were one joined hub of brainpower. That way, each of us could cover a quadrant of the sky.

It wasn't ten minutes before Ope yelled, "Fire!" and we all looked east. I missed it but I heard the click of his tally counter. He was the meteor-counting champion. Game on!

"Fire!" yelled Ope, again, and I caught it, too, out of the corner of my eye. Click.

We were in the heart of the meteor stream. When the timer on my phone signaled an hour had passed, I had counted seventeen. Ope was tops with twenty-three and it wasn't even midnight. Soon they'd be coming fast and heavy.

And then we heard the cars.

"What's that?" said Artie.

"Whaddya think?" I said.

"They sound close," said Ricardo nervously.

They did sound close, just like last night.

"My brother knows these guys who do pop-up hot-rod racetracks," said Ric.

"Where?"

"Anywhere. They don't care."

"Like, on private property?"

"Sure. Someone comes, they take off."

"But at night?"

"Less chance of getting caught," said Ric.

"Also, way more risky," said Ope.

"They wouldn't do it if there were sheep, would they?"

"These guys," said Ric. "They'd do anything for a kick. They're the same guys who race their snow-mobiles on the lake in late March."

"A dying breed," said Ope.

The cars revved and squealed — two at least, but maybe three or more. Even over the engine sounds we could hear shouts and laughter.

"They sound closer than the back meadow," said Ric, sounding more nervous than ever. I'd been thinking the same thing.

"The high meadow's where I'd do it," said Artie. "There's hazards everywhere: boulders and old rotten barbed-wire fences —"

"Not to mention trees," said Ope.

"It'd be killer," said Artie.

"Let's hope so," said Ope. Then he yelled, "Fire!" And clicked his counter. He was the only one who caught it — the only one still lying on his back looking up. It was just too hard to concentrate with all the noise. My brain was working overtime.

"They sound drunk as skunks," said Ric. He sounded frightened.

"How can you tell?" said Artie.

"You've met Ric's brother," said Ope.

It was true. Ricardo got the brains in his family. His older brother got all the alpha male idiot genes. The laughter was a long way off but it did sound kind of boozy.

"They'd never make it up the trail, would they?" said Ric. "I mean as far as the house?"

Not in a car, I thought. We bush-hog the trail all the way to the old train bed, but it's pretty rocky.

"Whoa!" said Artie suddenly, and we all caught it — a fireball — hurtling to Earth and disappearing into the trees.

"That was huge!" said Ric.

And then we heard the unmistakable sound of a car crash.

"HOLY ROMAN Empire!" said Artie.

Even Ope was climbing to his feet now with

a hand from me and Ric. I raced up the lawn, up the stairs to the deck and looked out over the bush.

"There's a fire," I said.

Artie joined me and climbed up on the picnic table. "You're right. Crap!"

Next came Ric who helped Ope up on account of he's so weak. The fire was flickering — a hot point of red in the deeper darkness of the forest.

"A direct hit!" said Artie.

"No way," said Ric.

"Highly improbable," said Ope.

"Then what is that?" said Artie.

"Ope's right," I said. "The sound was metal on metal. Probably one of the cars rammed into another one."

"Or a *metal* meteorite the size of a basketball crashed into a car," said Artie.

"We'd have probably felt it," said Ope.

"I think I did," I said. The others looked at me, surprised. "I felt something, anyway."

"What do we do?" said Artie.

"Call 911," said Ric, already taking his phone out of his pocket.

"The fire brigade are volunteers," said Artie. "They'll take forever to get here."

"I can't get a signal, anyway," said Ric. "I'll try the house phone." He turned at the door to the living room. "Maybe we should, you know, go inside? Lock the doors?"

"It's not the zombie apocalypse, Ricardo," said Artie. Ric glowered at him.

"What if the bush catches fire?" I said.

"There was a thick dew," said Ope. "Remember when we laid down our sleeping bags?"

"Yeah, but it's been —"

"Shhh!" said Artie. And we listened. The guys out there were screaming at each other. It sounded like a fight. Then one car roared into action and went squealing off — the other way, from the sound of it. Had to be. Then another car took off and a third.

"Maybe it *is* the zombie apocalypse," said Artie.

"Better phone," said Ope.

"I'm on it," said Ric.

And as he was closing the door, I shouted, "Wait!" I raced after him into the house and while he went to use the phone in the kitchen, I raced up the stairs to my room. There was a lot of forest in the way, but from there I could see the fire better. Pinpoint it.

"Got any idea where it is?" said Artie. He'd followed me, all out of breath.

"Yep. You were right. It's out on the high meadow, right near You and Me Pal Hill."

He joined me at the window. The fire was burning hot, flames leaping up into the night.

Artie looked at me and some of that distant glow was in his eyes. "You wanna?"

I nodded. And we took off downstairs.

"You are totally nuts," said Ric.

"It'll probably just burn out," said Ope, who was on his back again, staring up at the heavens, counter in hand. "The grass will be wet and there's no wind." Then he glanced at Artie and me. "Besides, I don't think those will make much difference."

We were armed with fire extinguishers. I had grabbed the one by the fireplace, Artie the one in the kitchen. They weren't all that big. We each had a heavy-duty Maglite, as well. We get a lot of blackouts where we live.

"Leave it to the pros," said Ope, turning his attention back to the sky.

"Yeah, but what if someone's hurt?" I had this vision of a body trapped inside a burning vehicle, writhing in pain. I *had* felt something — something deep in my gut. "I'm going," I said.

"Me, too," said Artie.

"Whoa!" said Ric. "Where'd you get that?"

Artie had a meat cleaver stuck in his belt. "It's in case of bears," he said.

"Bears?" said Ric.

"Or aliens," said Artie. "I mean, who says it wasn't a UFO that crashed out there?"

Ope groaned with disdain. "Clearly there's no intelligent life around here," he said.

"Ope's right," said Ric. "You're being stupid."

"I didn't exactly say that," said Ope.

"I'm still going," said Artie, and we started off.

"Hold on," said Ric. "Emergency services said to wait right here."

"So, you guys wait," I said, and then Artie and I took off into the dark.

"I'll go out to meet them at the head of the driveway," Ric shouted after us.

"Excellent," I shouted back.

"Thirty-eight," said Ope. It was the last thing we heard as we jogged down the pathway that led from our backyard to the trail.

The trail was rough, overgrown since we'd last bush-hogged it, and laced with fallen branches. I'd never come out here at night, and if it hadn't been for Artie I'd have turned back. Why did he have to say that about bears? Mostly we trained our flash-lights on the ground, but every now and then I flashed mine into the underbrush to either sides of the trail, looking for a darkness that was thicker than the night. With more fur.

"Ope's going to destroy us with his meteor count," I said.

"Yeah, but we'll be the ones who make the big discovery," said Artie. "We'll be famous."

We slopped through a low spot, inky water lapping at our ankles.

"What did you feel?" said Artie.

I tried to think how to describe it. "Like the earth shifted," I said.

"Got to be a UFO," said Artie. "Glad we've got our phones."

I didn't bother reminding him that the chance of getting a signal was zilch.

THE LOW meadow was a real slog. Mud squelched underfoot, seeping into my sneakers. Artie tried jumping from one grassy tuft to the next. Then he fell with a splash.

"Ow!" he said.

"You okay?"

"Sure. I just said 'Ow!' for something to say."

I helped him up. "Can you walk?"

He took a step, grimaced but nodded.

Then we climbed a short hill to drier ground and the grove of trees that stood sentinel there. We called it the Squad. We'd mapped every part of the high meadow. From here we could see the fire up ahead on the rise where we built a fort a couple years back: You and Me Pal Hill. It was a car, all right, still blazing, black smoke pouring into the still night air.

"Look at this," said Artie. He was standing in an area flattened and torn up by muddy tire tracks. We followed the tracks through the prickly ash that dominated the slope, managing to avoid getting too scratched up.

And then we were there, close enough to feel the heat and hear the crackle. Some old clunker, the paint bubbling and blistering on its sides, the front passenger door hanging open.

Crouching low, we pulled up to within ten meters of it, which was as close as we could get because of the heat. I wiped the sweat from my face and peered into the vehicle. Didn't seem to be anyone or anything inside. There was a stench in the air and Artie started coughing. What little breeze there was this high up pushed the smoke our way and we stumbled around the fire in a wide perimeter to get upwind of it.

Carefully we walked, keeping our distance, aiming our flashlights this way and that to see if there was anyone lying nearby. I glanced at Artie. He'd drawn his cleaver, which made me nervous. The ground was rocky — rocks some farmer had piled here a hundred years ago. We stood looking at the front of the car.

"It's stoved in," said Artie.

"So, not a meteorite hit," I said.

He shrugged — didn't want to give up on the dream just yet.

"Somewhere in the valley, there'll be some crappy old beater like this one with a stoved-in back end or side or maybe even front end — a head-on collision."

"Maybe," said Artie. "But maybe it was when he got hit by the meteorite that he crashed into the other guy."

When we got to the driver's side, I was sure we'd see a body lying facedown on the trail, his back charred to a crisp as if our high meadow was some war-torn place. I had my extinguisher at the ready — but there was no one there.

By then we could hear, over the crackling of the fire, the sounds of sirens way back on the road to my place.

I shoved the flashlight into my pocket and walked toward the car, the fire extinguisher raised.

"Isn't that kind of like attacking Optimus Prime with a pair of pliers?" said Artie.

I looked at the extinguisher, looked at the car. "It's just that I've always wanted to use one of these things."

I turned to Artie. He looked red in the reflected light. "Knock yourself out," he said. "But I was just thinking how the car might blow."

I hadn't thought of that. It usually did in movies. I backed up in a hurry — so fast I fell over. Which started Artie laughing. I scrambled to my feet and it was only then that I saw the boy.

"Artie?" I said standing and staring.

"What? Whoa!" He'd seen him, too.

We aimed our flashlights at the kid and he covered his eyes.

"That hurts!" he said.

"Sorry!" we both said at the same time and aimed our flashlights down at the foot of the stump where he was sitting, about twenty meters uphill from the burning car. A preschooler, by the look of him, wearing pajama bottoms and a ratty T-shirt, clutching a pathetic piece of blankie.

"What … what are you doing here?" I said.

"He told me to wait," said the boy.

"Who?"

"My daddy." He yawned. "He said to wait and NOT TO MOVE." He waggled his finger at us, just like his dad must have done to him. "'Cause it would be DANGE-ER-US."

We walked up to the copse of three rock elms. There were boulders and high grass all around him. A slip of breeze found us. I shivered but it wasn't just from the wind.

"Are you cold, little guy?" I asked.

The boy nodded. I put down my Maglite and fire extinguisher and slipped off my hoodie. "Here," I said. "Put this on." I helped him with it. He was swamped in it — covered right down to his flip-flops. "Is that better?"

As soon as he'd recovered his blankie, he nodded again. Then he pointed at the burning car. "That's my daddy's," he said.

Artie and I exchanged a secret glance and turned to look again at the car. Artie muttered something under his breath. If he'd been at his place and his mother was nearby, he'd have had to put a dollar in the swear jar.

With another glance at each other, I grabbed up my flashlight and headed down to take a closer look. As I got nearer, I held up my arm to ward off the heat. From about three or four meters away, I stood on my tiptoes, trying to peer into the shattered driver's side window. Then I backed off, quick.

"Empty," I muttered. And Artie and I both breathed a shaky sigh of relief.

"Daddy got banged," said the boy. "His friends took him away."

"And they left you here?"

He nodded. "They didn't remember."

"Wait," said Artie. "They drove off with your dad and they just left you?"

The boy nodded again and then grasped his blankie closer. "Mommy said Daddy had to look after me — he PROMISED — but he forgot and she said SHE wasn't looking after me and then they had a BIG fight and she left. So, Daddy said we were going to have some fun. Only when we got here, he told me to sit and NOT TO MOVE." He waggled his finger again.

Artie and I stared at each other. His jaw was hanging open. I think maybe mine was too.

Then the car exploded.

THE FIREMEN came, the cops, the whole emergency response team. We met them just as they were crossing the swampy lower meadow, me carrying the boy, Artie carrying everything else. The firemen and cops raced up the hill toward the fire. I told the paramedics what the kid had told us, that they'd taken the injured guy with them.

"Nobody in the vehicle?" said the male paramedic. I said, "I sure hope not," and he decided to go check, leaving his partner with us.

I have a feeling the kid would have given us a fight about leaving his stump, if it hadn't been for the explosion. He pretty well leapt into my arms and clung there, and I clung to him so hard it was kind of hard to say who was clinging to who. Even the other paramedic couldn't peel him off me and I said I was okay and the kid was okay, and she said as long as you're sure and I said I'm sure, it's fine, and so I got to carry him all the way home. The paramedic kind of guided me by the arm through the boggiest part. She sure had a strong grip.

Just before we reached the shelter of the trees and the head of the trail, the kid said, "Look!" He was pointing over my shoulder across the meadow up at the sky. I caught the tail end of a fireball.

"A shooting star," he said.

"That's right, a meteor."

"Mee-tee-or," he said.

"Yeah," I said.

"There's lots of mee-tee-ors," he said.

"There are tonight," I said, hoisting him up a bit so he was sitting more on my hip. His skinny legs coiled around me, tight.

"I saw them," he said.

"Yeah?"

"Yeah, lots and lots and lots of them. Maybe ten."

"That is a lot."

The boy looked at me. "I'm this old," he said and held up his hand right in front of my eyes, with his thumb folded over his palm. Then he threw his counting hand around my neck and rested his head on my shoulder.

"You tired?" said the paramedic. I was but I shook my head. She went ahead with a big flashlight, while Artie walked beside me, lighting our way.

"That feeling you had?" he said. I glanced at him, waiting for him to finish the thought, but he just looked at me as if he was waiting for me to finish it for him.

"What time is it?" I asked.

He managed to hoist his phone out of his pants' pocket. Showed it to me: 11:43. I nodded. There was still a chance that my brother might be born today. Maybe he had been born already.

Artie fell back a step. "The kid's asleep," he said, real quietly. "He must weigh a ton."

"Yeah, but it's okay." My mind was working overtime. I was wondering if Ricardo might make this little space cadet a micro necklace. Maybe he could make two.

CHRISTMAS WITH AUNTIE ANNIE PING-PONG

Auntie Annie Ping-Pong had lost her marbles.

It used to be fun. Annie used to feed him Welsh cake and shortbreads and Coke, which he wasn't allowed at home. Then they would play cards or watch soaps and boo the bad guys. But not anymore. No more baking; his father had taken the fuses out of Annie's stove so she couldn't hurt herself. And no more cards; Annie thought all the cards were people. One day she had a long conversation with the three of clubs.

Auntie Annie Ping-Pong wasn't a real name, but she had always been that to Matt. And now, when he thought about it, it seemed perfect. Talking to Annie was like a ping-pong match. They could keep the ball in the air for only so long, before *plop!* it would roll off the table — *zing!* it would bounce off the ceiling — *flub!* it was snagged in the net.

"Don't let it get you down," said Matt's father. "At least these hallucinations of hers are friendly."

They were friendly, all right. He watched Annie place a little lavender-colored pillow behind a fruit bowl. "Are you comfy, dear?" she asked. She patted a shiny Northern Spy on the head.

"You're talking to an apple," said Matt, trying to sound patient.

Annie smiled at him and then smiled at the apple, too, as though they were all having a good time together.

Her neighbors in the condo were great. She left her door unlocked and they popped in for visits.

"She came around to our place today," said Mr. Morcombe to Matt one afternoon. "Seems her 'visitors' were sleeping in her bed and she couldn't take a nap. So I sent them packing."

"Thanks," said Matt. He smiled respectfully.

"No problemo," said Mr. Morcombe. "We all love our Annie."

Which is when Matt thought a horrible thing: "If you all love her so much, why don't *you* keep her." Of course, he didn't say it. These days he was full of things he didn't dare say.

He took to sneaking around to Annie's back door to avoid neighborly confrontations. Auntie Annie lived on the ground floor. There was a deck with steps down to the garden. She seldom went out anymore, not even to church. And she never went out alone.

"I'm a little uncertain on my pins," she said leaning heavily on her walker. Matt remembered when he had to run to keep up with her. It made him sad.

Some days were worse than others. Once, he arrived after school to find her at the counter in the kitchen. "You're here," she said, with relief. "My muscles are on holiday, today, Matt. Perhaps you can cut this sandwich."

"Sure thing," said Matt and helped her to a seat at the table.

But he couldn't cut the sandwich. Because, apart from cheese, lettuce, mayonnaise and tomato, the sandwich also contained the TV remote. It was a TV remote sandwich with the works! Matt didn't say anything. He took out the remote and handed her the sandwich cut up into quarters. She took a bite and looked thoughtful. "Hmmm, it seems to be missing something," she said.

"Don't laugh," said Matt to his parents at dinner that night. "Can't they give her some drug or something?"

"She's already on a dozen drugs," said his father. "The side effects of the drugs are part of the problem. Especially the prednisone for her temporal arteritis. But without it, she might have a stroke."

Matt pushed his potatoes around on his plate gloomily. He had spent half an hour trying to get the gunk out of the TV remote. When Annie asked him what he was doing, he said, "I'm digging cheddar cheese out of your TV remote, Auntie Annie."

"Oh," she said, chuckling merrily. "That sounds fun."

"Shouldn't she be in a home, or something?" said Matt irritably. "Then she would have real people to talk to instead of talking to the furniture. Or making sandwiches out of it."

His mother patted his hand. "I know it's weird, but try to see the bright side of it. She's got a care worker coming in twice a day, Meals on Wheels bringing her hot lunches, and good neighbors. As long as her delusions are harmless, she's just as well off where she is."

But Matt wasn't so sure her delusions were harmless. Some days she was pretty jumpy.

"It's these guests," she said to him one cold November afternoon. "I can't get them to leave. What am I going to feed them?"

Matt got an idea. "Your guests are imaginary," he said softly. "They can make their own imaginary food."

She looked pleased, but then she frowned. "Well, just as long they don't make any smelly stuff like fish."

December rolled around. It snowed and every fat flake whispered Christmas. When Matt arrived at the condo one day, he found Auntie Annie out on her porch with just a sweater over her shoulders, staring at the garden and the river beyond. Quickly, he hustled her inside and wrapped a blanket around her. She kept staring out the window, preoccupied.

"What's up?" he asked.

She looked confused. "Is this a test?" she asked, her teeth chattering. "I've had so many tests lately."

"No," said Matt, "it's not a test."

But she wasn't listening, she was thinking. Then she smiled. "I know," she said. "Gloria Boemkamp is up. I can hear her walking around." She beamed with pride. She made Matt listen, and sure enough, Mrs. Boemkamp was walking around upstairs. Matt shook his head, tried not to scream with frustration and took himself off to watch TV in Auntie Annie's bedroom. He couldn't cope.

A few minutes later she was at the bedroom door wringing her hands.

"What is it?" Matt asked, a little frightened by the look on her face.

"They're still there," she said. "I think we had better invite them in."

"Who?" said Matt.

"The two fellows at the bottom of the garden by the river. They've been there all day. They must be very cold."

Matt went to look. Auntie Annie followed him. "Oh," she said. "There's three of them now."

The river bank was empty but for the tall grass and cattails dusted with new snow. Annie opened the sliding door. A gust of icy wind came in and shook the snow off its boots. Matt closed the door quickly. But not quickly enough. Annie was already addressing her latest guests.

"Did you come by boat?" she asked.

The three imaginary strangers were still there the next day. None of them had drunk their tea, but Annie was in high spirits. "They didn't like plain old everyday tea," said Auntie Annie to Matt when he arrived that afternoon. "So I brewed them a pot of Lapsang souchong."

She didn't seem anxious anymore, but Matt was. "Do you think it's wise to let strangers in?" he asked, trying to be diplomatic.

Annie looked toward the china cabinet. Apparently, that was where the three men congregated. She had offered them a seat, she told Matt, but they had things to talk about in private.

"Well, I wouldn't normally, of course," said Annie. "But you see, they have to wait somewhere. And I feel I almost know them," she added.

"Wait for what?" said Matt. It sounded ominous to him.

But Annie only looked delighted. "For Christmas, Matt. What else?"

"Why didn't I think of that?" said Matt.

Then Annie excused herself. "Which reminds me," she said as she motored off in her walker. "I'd better get started on my knitting."

She returned with her knitting bag. Matt hadn't seen her knit in ages. Her arthritis was usually too bad. Now she seemed raring to go. "What do you think?" she said, taking her favorite seat by the window. "Blue or pink?" She held up two thick balls of pastel-colored yarn.

Matt was at a loss. "What do *they* think?" he said gesturing toward the china cabinet.

Annie laughed. "Oh, them," she said, dismissing the strangers with a wave of her hand. "They could care less about knitting." Then she dug out a ball of creamy white wool. "I'll go with white," she said. "Better safe than sorry."

"Annie?" said Matt. "What would you say if I told you I don't see anyone in the corner. No one at all."

Annie looked at him with kindly eyes. "I'd say you should see someone about your vision."

"How about I walk home after school from now on?" said Matt to his mother in the car that night. This was a joke. They lived in the country, twenty kilometers from Annie's condo. "I just can't keep up!" he cried.

"Christmas is coming," said his mother trying to cheer him up. "Auntie Bridget and her family will be here and you'll get a well-deserved break."

"Annie's already got more visitors than she can handle," said Matt. He stamped his foot. "Why can't I convince her they're not real?"

They drove in silence for a moment, the snow swirling into phantom forms in the darkness before them. And then Matt's mother said, "Well, they are real to her, Matt. It's hard to argue with someone about something they can see with their own eyes." Matt didn't respond. Then his mother said, "She's in such a good mood. And knitting, too. Play along if you can, okay?"

Matt turned to the back seat piled high with groceries. "You hear that, guys?" he said. "We've got to play along."

His mother laughed. "That's the spirit," she said.

And he did play along.

Auntie Annie Ping-Pong was deep in conversation with the three strangers when Matt arrived the next day. "They're magicians," she said.

Matt waved at the china cabinet. "Hi, guys?" he said. "Can you do disappearing tricks?"

"I'm sure they can," said Annie, knitting away, her gnarled fingers going a mile a minute. "They were doing card tricks earlier. And one of them, Gaspar, he made a gold coin come out of my ear."

"Casper," said Matt. "The friendly ghost?"

Annie laughed. "Don't be silly, dear. I said Gaspar. And the tall one is Balthazar and the other's got such a thick accent I can't get his name, so I just call him Norman. Now, why don't you go see how the others are doing?"

The others.

The TV was blaring in Annie's bedroom. Wrestling was on. Matt watched for a moment as Goldilocks Gabor pinned Herod the Horrible to the floor. Then Matt noticed that there were cups of tea strewn all over the bedroom. And plates of cookies. There was even a plate on the floor. He picked up one of the cookies. It was still warm. It was one of Annie's shortbreads, a little too brown on top but good.

In the kitchen, he checked the oven; it wasn't hot. But the toaster oven was.

"Good cookies," said Matt rejoining Annie in the living room.

She smiled appreciatively, the skin around her eyes crinkling. "You're kind to say so," she said. "They're a little dry. But you see, I had to do something, with all these new folks arriving. And their dogs, too."

"Ah, dogs. That explains the cookies on the floor."

She nodded. Then she stopped knitting for a minute and looked puzzled. "What are those things that go *Baaaaa*?" she asked.

"Sheep," said Matt.

"They might be sheep," said Annie.

"Sheep," said Matt again. *Hmmm,* he thought. This was getting interesting. He sat at Annie's feet, watching her knit, and said, "That looks like a blanket, is somebody having a baby?"

"That's what they say," said Annie gesturing with her busy needles toward the three strangers.

"The magicians," he asked.

"That's right," said Annie.

"Sort of like wise men," said Matt.

"Oh, they certainly seem so," said Annie. Then she leaned forward and whispered to Matt, "Actually, they can be a bit snooty at times." Matt snickered and Annie admonished him to keep quiet. "They've probably got a lot on their mind," she added.

"I bet," said Matt.

Annie's eyes twinkled. She had once been a first-class twinkler. Matt had almost forgotten. Her eyes usually looked foggy lately on account of all her medication. But they looked twinkly now, and it was as welcome to Matt as the smell of baking. Suddenly, he felt good. He had a pretty good idea what was going on and he was full of things he *could* say. "The ones in the bedroom watching wrestling: Do you think maybe they're shepherds?"

Annie paused. "Yes," she said. "Except I think one of them said he was an electrician. Oh, and I just remembered," she added excitedly. "Some of them are angels, Matt. You just ask."

Matt nodded. "Figures," he said. "I mean with the wings and all." And then he had a great idea. "So how about we make them something special?"

Matt put the fuses back into the oven and set it at the right temperature for angel food cake. It was one of Annie's specialties. She didn't need a recipe. She hummed a little song while she worked and she got around fine on her pins, Matt noticed. He separated eggs. It wasn't easy.

When Matt's mother came, they had to wait for the cake to finish baking. Matt introduced his mother to the wise men and the gang in the bedroom who were watching *The Simpsons* now. The Christmas special.

FINALLY, INEVITABLY — although it always seemed to take forever — Christmas Eve day rolled into town. Matt's father's sister Bridget arrived from Winnipeg. A limp and wretched little tree was found in town and made presentable with decorations. Presents appeared from nowhere to go under it. Annie looked flushed and a little perplexed. "It's going to be very crowded," she whispered to Matt. He knew what she meant.

Then Bridget said, wouldn't it be nice if they all went to Midnight Mass together. Annie had to sit down. She looked bewildered. "Oh, but I can't," she said.

"Please come," said Bridget. "You always love that service."

Annie started wringing her hands. She appealed to Matt.

"It's okay," he said, taking her hand. Then he explained to Bridget and her husband, Bob, and his cousins Ray and Sylvia why Annie had to stay behind.

His cousins looked around them with alarm as if hanging out with a bunch of shepherds and sheep — even imaginary ones — wasn't their idea of a good time. "You sort of get used to it," said Matt understandingly.

At Annie's suggestion, he introduced everyone to the wise men, the shepherds, the sheep, the angels and the electrician. Then everybody went to church. Everybody except Auntie Annie Ping-Pong and Matt. They stayed behind and waited, Annie at the window, Matt pacing.

Then, a little after eleven, with a gasp of delight, Annie flung open the sliding door.

"You two must be bushed!" she said as she welcomed the invisible travelers into her house. Matt watched with fascination as Annie led her guests to the bedroom, making small talk the whole way, about the weather and the trip and taxes and how Mary was holding up. Matt found himself suddenly wishing he could see what she could see.

He sat there alone by the Christmas tree. After a bit he got up and went to the door. It was a cold night. He thought maybe he'd better let the donkey in or give it some hay or something. He laughed to himself. Here he was playing the game. It was easier when you knew the story, knew the players. Christmas gave him a script. What would happen after Christmas? There was a lot of life left in Annie. Oh well, he thought. Whatever. But he knew he would keep finding the ball and putting it back in play: ping-pong, ping-pong, ping-pong.

There was no donkey on the deck. Of course not. But there was a winter moon and a fresh supply of air gift-wrapped with stars. Revived and shivering, Matt stepped back into the delicious warmth of Annie's apartment.

He went to check up on her. She was sitting in a corner of her bedroom lit by a dimmed lamp, her hands folded together under her chin, staring lovingly at the blanket she had made, which lay in the middle of her bed. Matt looked at the bed. There was no one there that he could see, no haloed child. But when he looked at Auntie Annie, there was a miracle all right. In her eyes.

Afterword

War at the Snow White Motel

One of the best times of my life as an author was writing the semi-autobiographical Rex Zero Trilogy, set in the Cold War of the early sixties. (*Rex Zero and the End of the World*; *Rex Zero, King of Nothing*; and *Rex Zero, the Great Pretender*.) I went on to write a fourth book in the series, but it just didn't work out. Happens. I've written several novels over the years that, no matter how much work I put into them or how many drafts I sweated over, just never were good enough to publish. Luckily, manuscripts like that still have some good bits in them, a passage here, a nice little chunk of dialogue there. Those manuscripts end up in my own personal literary wrecking yard, ready to be repurposed one day. That's what happened to the opening chapter of the book I was going to call *Rex Zero in Deep*. I reworked it to make this story and I think it turned out just fine.

You can read about what happened on August 4, 1964, on Wikipedia. The "incident" that did or didn't happen brought about the "The Gulf of Tonkin Resolution," which gave the president of the United States, Lyndon B. Johnson, the legal justification to start open warfare against North Vietnam. Skip tells Rex that hopefully the war could be over "real soon," but the truth was it didn't end until 1975.

Like Rex, I spent quite a number of summers in Ocean Park, Maine, and we sometimes stayed in motels en route, though never one quite like the Snow White! I think 1964 might have been the last summer we went to Maine, but I have no idea what dates we were there. I can't help thinking how eerie it would be to arrive somewhere for a holiday just as that country went to war.

Ant and the Praying Mantis

One of the most troubling, hurtful, even frightening things that can happen to you is being accused of something you didn't do — or didn't realize you were doing. Yes, you did *something*, but not what you're being accused of and it's all so complicated. When Ant tells the principal that he didn't do what she alleges, she says, "Oh, you did," as if it's black and white in her mind, as if she hasn't heard a word he's said in his defense. He gets up to leave and she says, "Excuse me, young man, you have *not* been dismissed," and he replies, "Yes, I have." He's not being rude, just telling the truth; she has dismissed him in that other sense — she has scorned him. I'm so glad Ant finds a way to really talk to Samantha and, through her, find something to stand up for. To stand tall.

Which brings me to the inspiring Greta Thunberg and her appeal to action on climate change. When I was trying to think of what could possibly raise Ant up from the personal despair in which he finds himself, I could think of nothing better than #FridaysForFuture. Samantha Grimsby-Paine is as blunt in her own passionate way as her Swedish heroine, and she's just the spur that Ant needs to get back on his feet again.

The Pledge

Sooner or later, every good friend I've ever had admits to some dumb thing they did when they were kids (or maybe just last week — let's face it, we never stop making dumb mistakes now and then). Typically, the story gets a good laugh, because it's usually not all that big a deal, nothing really awful. And yet, it was a big deal when it happened. Excruciating. It's amazing how you never quite get over the niggling feeling of embarrassment — sometimes shame — even decades after the incident. Part of the problem, I guess, is that you seldom get the chance to really apologize or pay back the person you did the dumb thing to. So the best you can do is pay it forward. Learn from the dumbness.

I guess that's why I wanted to give Joe and Danny a chance to live up to this pledge they made to each other. I'm kind of guessing Joe only came up with the whole idea to calm Danny down, not really thinking the opportunity would ever truly arrive to do the right thing, make amends. What's particularly worthy in my estimation is that they still could have easily gotten away with doing nothing and yet they fulfill their pledge anyway. Nice.

The Journey to Ompah

I live in Eastern Ontario, on seventy-six acres of bush and high meadow, with only a rind of topsoil. It's not very arable, but I love the roughness of the landscape, with the rock punching through everywhere like an angry, old, giant prisoner, buried alive. There's a line I heard once when we moved to these parts: if you see a rock you can take it for granite.

Place figures prominently in my writing. I love to ground a story in a real landscape; it often seems almost like a character to me. In this story, I created Michel's grandfather out of a chunk of granite. He's all sharp edges and heft. Unforgiving.

Three of my novels are set in the fictional town of Ladybank. You'll also see it mentioned by name in "The Pledge." The truth is that Ladybank is Perth, Ontario, and the landscape featured in most of these stories is Perth and its vicinity, where I've lived for the last thirty years. Fictionalizing a place allows you to add a store here or a street there or move the river over a little, if you feel like it. But the landscape — the blood and bones of it — isn't fictional. To me, landscape is never simply setting. The word "setting" always makes me think of the backdrops in school plays, painted on paper and kind of just hanging there, pretending to be a field or the ocean, fluttering a bit when you walk past. For me, setting isn't enough; I want the land to evoke a sense of place. I have this funny feeling we all become a little of where we live.

In a House Built Out of Dragonfly Wings

This story was written twenty-five years ago, which is an interesting coincidence, since it was commissioned for a book celebrating twenty-five years of Greenpeace. That anthology, *Beyond the Rainbow Warrior*, is a collection of stories that look at environmentally relevant issues from a lot of different angles. It's good to see my own contribution reprinted again, although it's a bit sad to realize that a quarter of a century on, we humans are still not doing enough to clean up our act. I like to think that imaginative souls like Jess can make a difference. In her flights of fancy, she turns her world into a place of magic and mystery — a place where toxic gunk has no place. Her passionate imagination gets turned into action. That's the best part.

I wasn't thinking about this story when I wrote "Ant and the Praying Mantis," but it's interesting to see a certain similarity in the duo of Jess and Walker compared to Ant and Samantha. What do they share? What makes them good partners?

Jack

I did find a frozen ermine in our garbage can. It was pretty amazing. We live in the country, and we keep the garbage in an out-of-service outhouse, just like in the story. Old Man Sunday is loosely modeled on a wood carver friend of mine, Michael, who does make remarkable animal figures. And yes, he does have a freezer full of dead creatures to use as models. He didn't kill them; people bring him what they find.

Several years ago, when I was heading to England, I asked Michael to make a stoat as a present for Philip Pullman. *The Golden Compass* and the other novels in the His Dark Materials trilogy are among my very favorite books of all time. I was going to be visiting Pullman when I was overseas and thought it would be nice to bring him a "daemon," like Lyra's dearest companion, Pantalaimon. In Lyra's world, a daemon is the external manifestation of a person's inner self and takes the form of an animal. Michael did an amazing job, and Pullman immediately put the stoat in his breast pocket — the kind of place a daemon would likely hang out if it was small enough.

241

As someone who suffered bullying as a kid, it's a subject that interests me. It's also a subject that gets written about a lot, and bullies in fiction can be too easily stereotyped. I wanted Dougal Ashur to be someone who was struggling himself. I wanted there to be a whole other motivation for his attention to the lead character. When Sunday says to the unnamed protagonist, "It's good to have a second set of eyes," I wanted to make a point about how sometimes we have to look at things differently — not jump to conclusions.

The Stuffed Toy

Years ago, I wrote a piece called "What Happened to Baby Roo?" for an adult collection of mystery stories called *Criminal Shorts: Mysteries by Canadian Crime Writers*. I used the same basic premise here, an otherwise ordinary old stuffed toy with a remarkable story behind it. The story is true, or at least the part about Christopher Robin leaving Roo in the crotch of a tree. What really happened after that … well, somebody knows, I guess, but not me. Which is what made it so delicious to make up a story. Twice. Hey, Mozart and Bach used certain themes and motifs over and over again in their music, so I figured it was okay. And the stories are really quite different.

You might like to read *The Enchanted Places*, Christopher Milne's book about being that very famous little boy. It's really interesting, especially if, like me, you love the Winnie-the-Pooh books. I'd say *The House at Pooh Corner* is still one of my top-ten favorite books of all time. If you only know the Disney movies, you might want to check out the real Pooh.

The Brotherhood of Interstellar Dirt

This whole collection of stories is dedicated to three of my writing buddies, who I don't get to see half enough. I've made them the three best friends of Noah, the central character of this story. Artie, Ope and Ricardo are, in real life, the talented writers Arthur Slade, Kenneth Oppel and Richard Scrimger … except, not really; they just share the same names. I didn't know these guys when I was a kid, but I sure wish I had. Bet they were a riot!

Like Noah, my birthday is August 12, and as far as I'm concerned, the Perseid Shower is my own very special birthday present from the universe. Thank you, universe.

What else about this story is true? Well, we do live on seventy-six acres of bushland, as I mentioned above, and we did once find a burned vehicle out in the middle of our property. It was a tractor. Never did find out who owned it or what it was doing there. The best thing about writing fiction is taking a curious or mysterious real experience and making up how it came about. And since it's fiction, you get to change the real experience any way you want. I mean, I could have written about a tractor from outer space crash landing, and the beginning of an attack on the Earth by alien farmers. Hmm, maybe I still will.

Christmas with Auntie Annie Ping-Pong

There was an Auntie Annie Ping-Pong in my family, but that was back in England, where I was born, and I never met her. As I was about to write this afterword, I asked my oldest sister who Ping-Pong really was, and she didn't remember. Anyway, it would be a great name to describe my own dear mum when dementia set in. She did have imaginary visitors all the time and mostly that was fine. It was no use trying to explain they were imaginary, although sometimes she found it frightening. I remember once saying to her, as gently as I could, "Mum, it's okay, they're only imaginary." To which she replied, "Oh, I know that, but do they?" That's a pretty amazing response.

Dementia can be really hard for a kid to experience in a beloved relative. It's hard for anybody. Suddenly this person you've known all your life is just not there anymore, not really. They haven't died — it's just that the light's on, but nobody's home. Or should I say, there's often this stranger who answers the door. All I could do in my mother's case was roll with it, which is what Matt does, as best he can.

TIM WYNNE-JONES is one of Canada's foremost writers for children. The author of over thirty-five books, he is a two-time winner of the Governor General's Award, as well as a two-time winner of the Boston Globe–Horn Book Award and the Arthur Ellis Award. His short-story collections include *Some of the Kinder Planets, The Book of Changes* and *Lord of the Fries*. He is also known for his Rex Zero series. Recently, he wrote the young-adult novels *The Starlight Claim, The Ruinous Sweep, The Emperor of Any Place* (which earned seven starred reviews) and *Blink & Caution*. Tim is also the recipient of the Edgar Award and the Vicky Metcalf Award for Literature for Young People. In 2012, he was made an Officer of the Order of Canada. He lives in Perth, Ontario.